The Swarm War

Rise and Ruin in the Xylos Expanse

Jason Thomson

Dedication

To the dreamers who stare at the stars and wonder what ancient truths lie hidden behind the silence.

To the fighters who question the past to forge a better future.

And to those who carry the burden of memory—may you never be forgotten.

Introduction

History is not written by the victors. It is written by the survivors. And in a dying galaxy, there are no victors left.

Under the light of a swollen, crimson sun, the once-mighty Kryll Imperium faces extinction. For generations, they have fought a losing war against the Zydonian Swarm—an endless, insectoid tide that consumes worlds and leaves only bone in its wake. Now, on the brink of annihilation, the last remnants of the Kryll fleet prepare for one final, desperate battle in the graveyard of their own dominion.

But the histories of the Kryll are built on lies. Beneath the battlefields and buried in the crust of forgotten moons, a secret slumbers. An ancient war was not ended, but paused. The Swarm they fight is not their true enemy. It is merely a veil, a prelude to a much deeper, more terrifying reckoning.

For in the silent spaces between stars, the true architects of reality wait. They are the Devourers, a cosmic force that considers the very existence of the Kryll a fracture in the universe that must be corrected.

This is the story of the end of one war, and the beginning of a truth. It is the story of Sergeant Xylar and the soldiers of the Kryll Marine Corps. They believe they are fighting for their homes and their history. They are about to discover they are fighting for memory itself. For when the old gods awaken, the only thing left to hold onto is the echo of who you were... and the choice of what you will become.

Contents

Chapter 1: Crimson Sunfall

The crimson sun of Xylos, swollen and dying, cast a blood-red haze over the void as the Kryll fleet prepared for a last, desperate push. Orbiting Xylos Prime, the Kryll Marine Corps—once the pride of the Imperium—hovered at the brink of extinction. Sergeant Xylar stood at the helm of the Razor's Kiss, a sleek Xy'lar-class marine assault dropship bristling with gravitic thrusters and neural-linked weapon pods. Through the viewport, the skeletal silhouettes of Kryll dreadnoughts loomed like funerary monoliths against the scattered bones of the Zydonian Swarm.

"Fleet Command to all Kryll Marine units," the comm crackled. "Initiate Phase Delta. This is our last window. Make it count."

Xylar's mandibles twitched in grim affirmation. His chitinous armor, black and ridged from decades of battle, clicked faintly as he turned to his fireteam. Five warriors, each clad in obsidian power-plate etched with unit sigils, stood ready. Neural filaments ran from their helmets into spinal armor ports—a direct interface with the ship's targeting and comms arrays. Kryll space marines were bred and trained for perfect synchronization.

"Form up," Xylar growled. "We're burning through the upper atmosphere in under two minutes. Jax, prime the dispersal pods. Valerius, monitor flank telemetry. We breach and secure the west ridge. No heroics."

Lieutenant Jax, younger and still too eager, gave a sharp salute. "Copy that, Sergeant. Dispersal pods charged and ready."

The Razor's Kiss shuddered as it punched through the outer thermosphere, trailing plasma. Zydonian flak streaked past, sizzling green bio-plasma that melted through lesser ships like acid rain. But the Kryll dropship was no fragile freighter. Its forward hull shimmered with kinetic deflection fields, and the gravitic armor layer beneath pulsed with counter-force buffers.

"Incoming cluster, starboard," Valerius reported. "Swarmers. Bio-signatures in the thousands."

Xylar gritted his mandibles. "Bring up swarm dispersal protocols. Pulse-mine grid active. Keep our trajectory tight. We're not breaking formation."

The Razor's Kiss swiveled with surgical precision, neural-linked guidance translating Xylar's micro-muscle movements into evasive arcs. Behind them, a Kryll destroyer took a direct hit—its hull torn open by a Zydonian boarding spike. A gout of flame and decompression ripped free, scattering marines into the void.

"That's the fifth cruiser in twenty minutes," Jax muttered.

"Focus," Xylar snapped. "We breach, we hold. Xylos Prime can't fall."

As the dropship neared insertion, the view shifted to the surface. Below, the ridgelines of Xylos Prime were overrun with Zydonian hives—massive bulbous growths sprouting towers of chitin and bone, surrounded by endless tides of insectoid warriors. Kryll defensive lines blinked red across the HUD—every perimeter buckling.

"Lock trajectory. Prepare for atmospheric burn," Xylar ordered.

A shriek erupted from the Razor's underbelly as retrothrusters fired. The marines locked into drop harnesses as gravitational compensators groaned under stress. The heat shield lit up, and then, with a roar, they were through.

Explosions peppered the landscape as other Kryll dropships hit ground. The Razor's Kiss slammed down behind a fractured ridgeline, skids grinding across blackened rock.

"Go! Go!" Xylar bellowed.

The hatch blew open, and Kryll marines surged out, weapons primed. Their plasma rifles, tuned for swarm disruption, fired in disciplined bursts, cutting swathes through the initial wave of Zydonian chitterlings.

Xylar led the charge, rifle blazing, his augmented HUD tracking multiple contacts. He ducked a bio-plasma bolt, returning fire with a burst that reduced the creature to a twitching smear of ichor.

"Squad Beta, flank left! Cut off that tunnel node! Jax, cover the ridge!"

The battle was chaos incarnate—a swarm of limbs, shrieks, and acidic blood. The Zydonians were faster now, more coordinated. Not just hive mind—directed. Xylar's gut twisted.

The Hive Queen had arrived.

He caught the signal spike on his neural relay. The psychic imprint was unmistakable: vast, cold, calculating. The queen wasn't just observing. She was directing.

"All units," Xylar barked over comms. "Queen presence confirmed. This isn't a defensive nest. It's a forward control node."

"Then we take it out," Valerius snapped. "Or we all burn."

They pushed forward. The swarm came from every angle—up from the tunnels, diving from cliffs, erupting out of fissures. Xylar's squad tightened formation, their HUDs linked in a tight combat net. Kryll marines fought like a single organism, each move calculated for maximum coverage and suppression.

A screech cut through the noise—Private Rell took a spike to the chest and crumpled in a spray of ichor. Jax dragged him behind a slab of broken metal and returned fire.

Rell gasped, choking. His final words were barely audible: "Hold the line... brothers."

Jax clenched his jaw. "You heard him!"

"Medic drone en route!" Valerius shouted, flinging a proximity flare that deployed a hovering triage unit from the dropship.

"No time! We move!" Xylar snapped. He didn't need to say it. They all knew: Rell was gone.

A memory surged unbidden—another ridge, another world. A younger Xylar hesitating to call the retreat. The cost: twelve marines lost to encirclement. He'd never hesitated since.

The squad hit the ridge's base under heavy fire. Zydonian gunners with acid launchers nested above, raining death. Xylar tapped his command node—a swarm-dispersal charge launched upward, detonating with a violet flash. Chitin and gore rained down.

"Breaching anchors set!" Jax reported.

Gravitic anchors thudded into the ridge wall, each magnetically stabilizing the slope as the team ascended under fire. The ridge burned under claw and cannon, but the Kryll climbed.

They reached the summit and beheld the super-node: a massive, pulsing hemisphere of neural tissue veined with glowing green arteries. Zydonian defenders ringed its base, and from its peak, tendrils snaked into the clouds—command relays for the Hive Queen.

"Valerius, pulse cannon ready?"

"Locked. Give me ten seconds."

"Jax, right flank suppression. Everyone else, hold this ridge!"

"For Xylos. For the Imperium. Until our blood is ash."

The phrase passed down the comm net like a rite. Even in the roar of battle, its weight landed.

A thundering roar split the sky—the orbital cannon, still in position above Xylos, had locked onto the Hive Queen's node.

"Target coordinates uploading now," Xylar said, his voice cold. "Hold the ridge until it fires."

The enemy came in waves. Marines fired, repositioned, and fired again. Explosions rocked the summit. Kryll bodies fell beside Zydonian husks. Xylar's arm sparked—his armor cracked. Blood streaked his visor.

Still he stood.

"Cannon locked," Valerius cried.

Xylar opened a final channel. "To all Kryll units: firestorm incoming. Brace or evacuate."

The sky turned white.

A beam of light, pure and searing, lanced down from orbit and pierced the node. It ruptured in a blossom of green flame, shockwaves flattening everything.

Xylar was thrown back. He hit the ground hard, the air gone from his lungs.

Silence followed.

Smoke. Ruin. The node was gone. So were half his men.

Jax limped to his side. "We did it."

Xylar looked to the sky. The sun bled crimson, the same color as the streaked ground around him.

"No," he said quietly. "We held. The war still burns."

He turned toward the ridgeline, where more Zydonian forces were beginning to stir amid the haze.

"And we burn with it."

The remaining Kryll marines regrouped, forming a loose perimeter as automated turrets began to unfold from the wrecked drop pods. Defensive protocols activated, locking onto heat signatures in the rubble.

Valerius limped over. "Command confirms secondary waves incoming. Reinforcements en route, but ETA is unknown."

"Then we dig in," Xylar said. He looked across the horizon, where green lightning flickered across low-hanging clouds. "This ridge doesn't fall. Not while we breathe."

Behind them, the sun dipped lower, casting the battlefield in deeper hues of blood and ash.

The first war cry of the second wave echoed in the distance.

And Sergeant Xylar raised his rifle.

"For Xylos. For the Imperium. Hold the line."

And the Kryll marines answered as one.

But even as their battle cry rang out, a low tremor rolled beneath their feet. Xylar froze. The marines glanced around—the sound wasn't from above. It was from below.

"Seismic activity?" Valerius asked, checking his sensor grid.

"Negative," Jax said. "It's coordinated movement. Subterranean."

Xylar's chitin flexed. "Zydonian tunnelers. New class. They're coming from underneath."

From the blackened ground, a massive Zydonian brute erupted—its body plated in obsidian chitin, four clawed limbs ending in fused drills. It screeched and hurled a cryo-core charge that shattered a nearby turret in frozen shards.

"New variant confirmed!" Valerius shouted. "Signal reads commander class."

Xylar activated his shock-baton and slashed across the brute's flank as it barreled toward the ridge. The Kryll marines formed a wedge around him.

"We adapt," Xylar growled, eyes narrowing. "We survive."

And as the brute fell, twitching, another sound echoed—not a roar, not a shriek, but a signal.

A repeating pulse.

Xylar turned to his HUD. The pattern wasn't Zydonian.

It was older.

Beneath the ruins of Xylos, something else had awakened.

The war was far from over. The Hive Queen had more tricks—and now, so would they.

Chapter 2: The Pulse Below

T he signal continued, rhythmic and unwavering, pulsing through the ash-laden ground beneath Xylar's boots. Not biological. Not Zydonian. The frequency was too precise, layered with harmonic tones—like it was encoded, designed. Ancient.

Xylar's HUD flickered as his neural interface struggled to process the anomaly. Static crawled along the edges of his vision, and somewhere beneath the hum of tech, a whisper—not audible, but sensed—murmured a name he did not recognize: "Vharnan."

"Valerius, triangulate the signal," Xylar ordered. "Jax, get those motion turrets recalibrated for subterranean targets."

The Kryll marine nodded and sprinted back toward the ridge's edge where their makeshift defenses hummed with low-energy warnings.

"Signal's coming from Sector Theta-Seven. Directly beneath the blast zone," Valerius replied, scanning through the distortion. "Depth—roughly 900 meters."

Xylar clicked his mandibles. "Too deep for standard seismic charges. We'll need to dig. Or descend."

Jax returned, rifle slung, mag-pack buzzing with over-clocked charge. "Dropship's burrower drone survived. Minor scarring. It can cut a shaft in under ten minutes."

"Deploy it."

Moments later, the Razor's Kiss's cargo bay released a heavy-duty drilling unit. The cylindrical automaton, covered in duranium spikes and grav-anchored, began melting a hole through the crust. Magmatic dust spiraled into the air, filling the sky with metallic haze.

"I don't like this," Valerius muttered. "This isn't recon. This is a tomb dive."

Xylar tightened the grip on his rifle. "Then we bring fire to the dead."

As the drone drilled deeper, strange readings blinked across their HUDs—pockets of null gravity, electrical flickers, bio-signatures that weren't alive. The air smelled wrong, even this far from the shaft.

Jax muttered to himself. "Feels like the planet's exhaling."

The descent shaft shimmered as the drone cleared the path. Xylar tapped his comms.

"Fireteam Alpha, with me. We go now. Valerius, Jax, perimeter is yours until reinforcements arrive."

Jax stepped forward. "Permission to accompany?"

Xylar hesitated. "No. You're next in line if I don't return."

He dropped into the shaft.

The ride was fast. The tunnel's edge was glassed smooth by the burrower's thermal array, reflecting the crimson glimmer of emergency lights embedded in the marines' armor. But as they descended deeper, the glow faded. Lights flickered. HUDs scrambled.

At the base: darkness.

The chamber was vast, its ceiling vanishing into shadow. Faint whispers swam through their neural links—not words, but pulses of thought and memory. One marine recoiled, gasping.

"Get it out of my head!"

"Hold formation," Xylar ordered. "Armor filters at maximum. Do not engage unless fired upon."

Then their sensors picked up structure. Not natural. Not Zydonian.

"Kryll design?" a marine asked.

"No... older. Look at the glyphs." Valerius ran his gauntlet across the obsidian wall. "Pre-Exodus markings. This is before recorded Kryll history."

The corridor opened into a circular atrium carved into black stone, seamless and silent. Runes ignited on the walls—not in red or green, but soft indigo. Then a platform lit up, revealing a floating orb: matte black, unmarked, suspended by unseen forces.

Xylar approached slowly, but before he could speak, a ripple passed through the chamber.

A defensive sentry emerged—silver, arachnid in form, legs clicking on stone. It lunged. Two marines fired, but the rounds phased through. Xylar dodged as a blade-like limb slashed the air.

"EMP burst!" he shouted.

One marine hurled a charge. The room flashed. The sentry froze, twitched, and then collapsed into dust as though it had waited eons just for that final moment.

"Now speak," Xylar said, turning back to the orb.

It responded—not aloud, but inside their minds.

"Designation: Kryll. Archive recognized. Defense sequence: disabled. Welcome, Legion-blood."

Several marines flinched. One dropped to his knees, clutching his helmet.

"What the hell is this thing?" another whispered.

Xylar's armor flickered. His gauntlet vibrated. That name again—Vharnan.

"Identify yourself," he said.

The orb pulsed. "I am Memory Core 917. I hold the legacy of the Ancients. You are out of time."

"Explain."

Instead of words, the orb unleashed visions into their neural links. A storm of memory.

Planets aflame. Stars fracturing under siege. Kryll fleets battling not the Swarm, but black ships shaped like razors and silence. Enemy soldiers made of shifting alloys. Creatures of pure logic. Worlds reduced to ash.

The marines cried out. One collapsed. Valerius grabbed him, shouting to bring him back.

Xylar stood still, trembling.

"This is... before the Imperium."

"The Devourers came," the orb said. "We buried what we could not kill."

Valerius's voice broke in on comms. "Sergeant—Swarm forces are falling back. Not attacking anymore. They're regrouping. It's... coordinated."

"They found this," Xylar said. "The Queen woke it up."

One marine stepped forward. "Sergeant, we should destroy the orb. We don't know what else it can unleash."

"No," Xylar said flatly. "We take it to Command. We need answers."

Beneath them, the ground trembled. Deep and sustained. The orb dimmed.

Jax's voice buzzed into their comms. "Sergeant. Orbital sensors show a mass rising from the dark side of Xylos. No transponder. Big. And we just lost comms with Sentry Grid Echo through Theta-Three."

Aboveground, Command scrambled. Sirens wailed in the CIC aboard the Razor's Kiss, and officers barked overlapping status reports.

"Unknown contact now in low orbit!"

"It's not broadcasting any ID. Should we engage?"

"Standby—launch all interceptors. Shields to full."

A nearby command lieutenant looked at the screen, pale. "That's not a ship—it's a platform. Or a node."

Fleet-wide alert protocols ignited. Automated sirens echoed across the surface command bunkers and into the ship decks orbiting overhead. Secondary officers relayed orders with clipped voices.

"All squadrons—lock and load. Orbital guns primed. We're not waiting for it to fire first."

"We've got a weapons signature—repeat, we have a spike on Deck Gamma!"

Valerius turned to Xylar, voice low. "You think it's one of them?"

Xylar looked at the orb, then the ceiling trembling above.

"I think we just stopped being the only ones fighting this war."

He looked at the orb.

"The war didn't end," he said. "It paused. And we just pressed play."

And beneath it all, the whisper came again: Vharnan.

A name. A warning. A key.

And maybe... a reckoning.

In that moment, standing in a chamber buried beneath a battlefield, Xylar felt something shift—not in the world, but in himself. The shape of history had changed, and he was no longer a soldier responding to war. He was now its herald.

Chapter 3: Ascension Protocol

The shaft walls screamed as the ascension harnesses engaged, propelling Fireteam Alpha upward through the glassed tunnel. Heat shimmered in the vacuum-cracked windows, seismic rumblings shook their harnesses, and warning lights strobed red. The orb—secure in its containment field—hovered between Xylar and Valerius.

"That thing wasn't built—it remembers being forged," Valerius murmured, eyes locked on the pulsating glow. Every few meters, their armor systems blinked with static interference. The orb pulsed like a heartbeat, dim but deliberate, as if sensing the surface drawing near.

Xylar's jaw clenched. He could still feel the echo of the vision, the heat of stars dying, the soundless war before history. A line from the Memory Core repeated like a curse: *They will awaken only if we fail again.*

"Surface readout shows seismic instability," Valerius called out. "Multiple fractures opened during our descent."

"Noted," Xylar replied. "Maintain tight formation. Orb goes topside—non-negotiable."

They emerged into the shattered surface of Theta-Seven. Black ash swirled around the crater rim, and Kryll gunships swept the horizon. Overhead, a tremor cracked the sky—deep red clouds split open as if bruised by something beneath.

Jax met them at the rim. "We have problems. High orbit is locked down. Something massive is climbing out of the planet's far side. Command's in scramble mode."

Xylar nodded. "Get that thing aboard the *Crimson Corsair*. I want eyes on it from space."

The retrieval dropship groaned overhead, anti-grav coils whining as it extended a boarding ramp. Xylar's fireteam ascended, orb in tow, the planet below trembling.

"Whatever this is," Xylar muttered to Valerius, "we just pulled the pin."

Aboard the *Crimson Corsair*, flagship of the 5th Kryll Battle Cluster, Commander Rhalyx leaned over the holotable with narrowed eyes. His chitin armor gleamed under pale command lighting. Dozens of holo-feeds surrounded him—fleet telemetry, seismic data, and a looping warning: **Sentry Grid Echo Offline**.

"All squadrons initiate Tier-Three Alert Protocol," barked Rhalyx.

"Tier-Three confirmed. Fleet-wide broadcast active," replied the tactical officer.

"Signal displacement pattern is expanding," another technician warned. "We're getting wake harmonics from the orbital fringe."

A junior lieutenant stepped closer. "Sir, the auxiliary carriers at the Helix Node are requesting direct orders. Their long-range sensors are detecting phase interference across three sectors."

Rhalyx's mandibles twitched. "Deploy cloaked recon corvettes. Full burn. And lock down the Specter logs—nobody outside this bridge sees those feeds until I say so."

The tension thickened. Holo-feeds flickered as emergency encryption cascaded through the fleet.

"We're not facing one relic," he muttered. "We're facing the ghosts of an entire war doctrine."

"What do we know?" he demanded.

"Object is approximately 1.8 kilometers in diameter," a technician replied. "Climbing through the stratosphere without propulsion. No identifiable drive signature. Origin point: subterranean layer Theta-Three."

"Is it Kryll?"

"Unknown. We suspect it's linked to the harmonic signal Fireteam Alpha recovered."

"Signal pattern?"

"Harmonic, resonant, matching no known encryption. It's... layered. Alive. It's also triggering echo patterns in dormant Kryll AI cores."

Rhalyx turned to the comms station. "Patch me to Xylar."

Xylar's HUD blinked as the channel opened. "Commander."

"You brought something onboard without clearance."

"I brought truth, sir. And we're running out of time to face it."

"Where is the artifact?"

"Secured in the forward vault. Monitored. Contained."

Rhalyx's mandibles clicked. "Prepare for full debrief. And for your sake, Sergeant, this better not be another Specter-class anomaly."

"It's not. It's worse. It's waking up the old ones."

In the containment bay, a team of armored Kryll scientists hovered over the orb, sensors and drones buzzing in coordinated harmony. The orb floated inside its stasis field, now faintly humming. Xylar stood watch with Valerius.

"Science team's prepping neural scan," Valerius muttered. "Not a fan of poking sleeping monsters."

"I gave strict parameters. Non-invasive only."

They watched as a drone approached the orb. The moment its scan array activated, the orb flared with blinding light. The lights across the containment bay went dark—then flashed crimson. Every Kryll present staggered. Xylar heard it again: *Vharnan.*

One scientist collapsed, convulsing. A feedback loop fried two drones midair. The orb's humming intensified, reverberating through the walls like an ancient song.

"Cut the scan!" Valerius roared.

The orb dimmed. Lights returned.

"Report!" Xylar demanded.

"Minor neural trauma," the lead scientist gasped. "The orb projected... something. A map? A memory? Not data—emotion. Grief. Rage."

Another medic emerged, scanning the collapsed Kryll. "Her synaptic activity spiked to 600%—it was like she lived through ten years of war in five seconds."

Xylar clenched a fist. "No more scans."

Valerius looked at him. "That thing remembers. And now it knows we're here."

In the Command Council chamber, Commander Rhalyx stood before a shimmering wall of senior fleet strategists. War-council protocols had initiated for the first time in six solar cycles.

"We've confirmed at least one object is emitting a signal echoing the Memory Core. It's not just a relic—it's a beacon."

An old war-priest leaned forward. "Long-range scans show micro-resonance trails between multiple sectors. This isn't an isolated event."

"We've seen this pattern before," another voice said. "Three fleets lost contact near the Helion Drift last cycle. We ruled it Swarm interference."

Rhalyx turned away from the display. "We were wrong."

The chamber dimmed as a real-time projection of Xylos appeared—three more pulse echoes appeared on the far hemisphere.

High above Xylos, the rising object finally breached the atmosphere. Plasma peeled off its hull like wax from fire. Its surface was black—not matte, not polished, but hungry. Absorbing. A void wrapped in armor.

Kryll interceptors were already en route. Three squadrons formed a net, weapons hot.

"Object has not responded to hails," said the squadron leader.

"Target lock," came the reply.

Missiles launched.

They didn't detonate.

As they neared the object, every warhead went dark—guidance systems dead. Fighters spiraled away, electronics scrambled.

"Retreat! Fall back!"

The object continued to rise. Silent. Intent.

On the orbital command deck of the Kryll flagship *Vigilant Aegis*, Admiral Kareth slammed a clawed fist against the command console. "Initiate Overwatch Protocol Zeta! Deploy the null-field satellites—now!"

"Satellites are scrambling, sir," a junior officer stammered. "But the uplink feed—it's already compromised."

Kareth watched as one by one, the satellites blinked out. No detonations. No trace.

"Gods of the Deep," someone whispered.

Kareth turned toward the command dome, voice hollow. "We've got nothing that can stop it."

The object kept ascending, its shape slowly rotating—revealing, at its core, a flickering network of glyphs glowing in harmonic rhythm. The same patterns found in the Memory Core.

Command's last line of defense had been erased in silence.

On the bridge of the *Vorrak's Lance*, a Kryll destroyer circling the planet's shadow side, Captain Enzor narrowed his eyes.

"Charge the beam-lance. Focus all relays through dorsal emitter. Let's see if this thing bleeds."

A searing lance of blue energy arced from the destroyer, cutting a swath through the sky.

The object didn't dodge.

Instead, it absorbed.

Then redirected.

A pulse of inverted energy snapped back toward the *Vorrak's Lance*. The ship didn't explode—it unraveled. Plates disintegrated, systems went dark, and the hull screamed in silence as it collapsed inward like a folding star.

Thousands of Kryll gone in a blink.

In the containment bay, Xylar staggered. The orb was glowing again, brighter this time.

"Sir, it's spiking!" a technician shouted.

Before he could respond, the world tilted.

Xylar stood on a battlefield—not the Corsair, not Theta-Seven. This was... older. The air was thick with ash and copper. The sky above was torn with red gashes of light. Biomechanical creatures—Swarm constructs—tore through trenches where armored warriors, Kryll-like but different, fell in droves.

He was seeing through someone else's eyes.

A soldier hurled a canister. Another wept as they activated a failsafe detonator.

He turned.

There were orbs—thousands—being buried in obsidian-lined chambers beneath the battlefield.

A voice echoed.

"They will awaken only if we fail again."

Then—

He gasped awake. The containment bay was intact, the orb dim again.

He wiped the sweat from his temples, breath ragged. The war wasn't a myth anymore. It was history—and it bled through him like it had been etched into his DNA.

Valerius grabbed him. "You were out for ten seconds. What happened?"

"They fought this war before," Xylar whispered. "They lost. And they left these behind... to warn us. Or maybe... to avenge them."

On the *Crimson Corsair*'s bridge, warning klaxons erupted.

"Power disruption. Deck 7. Unauthorized energy spike."

Rhalyx spun toward his tactical officer. "What's on Deck 7?"

"Backup vault. Artifact containment."

"No other orbs were brought aboard—"

"Then it's not ours."

Xylar's gauntlet vibrated. He looked down. The orb pulsed—once.

"CommandNet interface request detected," a warning AI intoned. **"Source: Memory Core 917. Do you authorize link?"**

"No," Xylar snapped. "Lock it down."

The orb vibrated harder. Containment field dimmed. Lights flickered. Then—silence.

Seconds later, the orb glowed softly and projected a singular image into his HUD: a vast chamber filled with hundreds of identical orbs. All dormant. All waiting.

And a message:

"One has risen. The rest remember."

Valerius stared, stunned. "It's calling them."

Xylar tapped his comms. "Bridge. Prepare for immediate fleet dispersal. We're not ready for what's coming."

Valerius pointed to the forward viewport. "Too late."

Beyond the clouds of Xylos, a second object crested the planetary curve.

Then a third.

In ancient archives, they were called Vharnan Spires—sentinels of forgotten ruin. But no one alive had ever seen one rise.

Then a fourth.

The sky, once empty, now brimmed with echoes of a forgotten war.

Rhalyx gripped the edge of the console, the weight of history pressing into his chitin.

For the first time in two decades of command, Rhalyx realized he had no counter-strategy. Just ghosts. And dread. *We thought we'd buried the past in myth and silence,* he thought. *But war doesn't sleep. It waits.*

Xylar stepped forward, heart thudding. "They're not responding. They're awakening."

He drew in a slow breath, voice low, certain.

"They buried them once. This time, they're rising. And we're not ready."

Chapter 4: Rise of the Echo

The command deck of the *Razor's Kiss* buzzed with sharp-edged tension. Officers snapped between terminals, issuing directives as warnings echoed through the comms. In the center of it all, Xylar stood with his gauntlet still stained in ash, the weight of the Memory Core slung in a containment field behind him.

Admiral Vekzara loomed over the tactical display, his translucent battle cloak pulsing with embedded rank glyphs. The elder Kryll's mandibles flexed with irritation as new data fed into the holotable.

"You brought it aboard?" he growled.

Xylar didn't flinch. "It spoke to us. Identified itself as Memory Core 917. Said it holds the legacy of the Ancients."

"And that justifies exposing our flagship to a relic that predates our recorded history?"

Valerius, flanking Xylar, interjected. "Sir, the orb referenced a threat—the Devourers. It showed us visions of them. Ships like blades. Creatures beyond comprehension."

Vekzara's eyes narrowed. "We've all heard the myths."

"They're not myths," Xylar said. "They're prelude. And that object rising from Xylos is their herald."

An ensign across the deck called out, "Contact is stabilizing in low orbit. Structure is now radiating harmonic frequencies identical to those detected below the surface."

"Weapons status?" Vekzara barked.

"No active weapons detected. But it's... growing."

"We just lost visual relay from Outpost Arc-6," another voice called out.

"Gone?" Vekzara barked.

"No debris. Just... phased out."

A silence stretched too long. Then Vekzara spoke again, voice quieter, like he was trying to contain the rising dread. "You have twelve hours."

Xylar stepped forward. "Permission to lead a boarding team. We need to see it up close."

Vekzara turned from the display, jaw rigid. "If that's truly a Devourer construct, it could assimilate anything that touches it. We're not risking another vector."

Before Xylar could respond, the orb behind him pulsed—dimly at first, then with a flash of blue-white light. Across the bridge, terminals spasmed, and screens filled with ancient glyphs.

"EMP shielding holding," a tech officer called. "But something's interfacing with our network. It's broadcasting into subroutines."

Xylar turned. "Memory Core 917. What are you doing?"

The orb hovered, spinning slowly. Its voice rang out across the minds of those present—not verbal, but clear.

"Accessing defensive schema. Calculating preservation probability."

The admiral roared, "Shut it down! Sever its feed!"

"It's not in our systems," Valerius said grimly. "It's in us."

Across the command deck, a dozen Kryll officers twitched—momentarily gripped by something unseen. Their eyes glowed faintly.

Then it stopped.

The orb dimmed.

"Preservation protocol suspended," the Core said. "Interference detected. Observing."

Vekzara's command cloak flared. "Xylar, get that thing off my ship. Now."

Xylar stiffened. "With respect, Admiral, we need it. The Swarm is backing off. Something worse is coming."

The admiral paused, staring at the orbital construct on the holotable. A slow, circular bloom had begun at its core, like a flower unfolding in silence.

"You have twelve hours. No more," he said finally. "Take the *Echo's Claw*. Recon the object. If it so much as whispers, burn it."

Across the fleet, war horns sounded. Defensive grids flickered to life. Autonomous dreadnoughts on the rim began silent countdowns. Yet none of it felt enough—not against this.

The *Echo's Claw* detached from the *Razor's Kiss*, its armor black and silent, bristling with electronic dampeners and null-void plating. Inside, Xylar stood with a squad of handpicked marines—Valerius, Rhalyx, Gheda, and Lorn.

As they approached the rising structure, its surface unfolded like living obsidian. No doors. No seams. Yet the ship slowed, drawn in by an unseen force.

"Engines idle," Gheda muttered. "We're being pulled."

Rhalyx growled. "Like prey into a nest."

Then, with a soundless pulse, an aperture irised open.

Xylar turned to his squad. "Weapons charged. Neural filters on full. We enter fast, form diamond, no stray steps. Valerius, watch the rear."

The marines nodded, nerves hard behind armored visors.

Inside, the structure was unlike anything Xylar had seen—walls that pulsed with memory, not light. Shapes moved through the stone, slow and uncertain, as if half-formed ideas were trying to take shape.

Etched into the floor in ancient Kryll script, a spiral enclosed in a circle pulsed faintly. Xylar didn't recognize it, but it thrummed in sync with his heartbeat.

At the heart: a column of light. Within it, a humanoid shape flickered. Not Kryll. Not Swarm.

"Is that... alive?" Lorn whispered.

Valerius' scanner pulsed. "No biometrics. No signal. It 's... projecting."

Suddenly the room bloomed with sound—not audible, but resonant. A deep harmonic that cracked visors and sent Gheda reeling.

Then the shape in the light turned.

It looked like a Kryll—older, thinner, the exoskeleton shaped with elegance rather than force. Its eyes held galaxies.

"What are you?" Xylar demanded.

The figure did not speak. But across every neural link, a single phrase was impressed:

"The war was never yours."

Then everything shattered.

Alarms blared in the *Echo's Claw*. Systems spiked, scrambled. Reality bent. One marine screamed and dissolved into mist, his atoms pulled apart by a force beyond energy.

"Fallback! NOW!" Xylar bellowed.

The aperture reappeared, and the marines launched out just before it vanished, the structure sealing behind them like it had never opened.

Back aboard the *Razor's Kiss*, Xylar tore off his helmet, gasping. Blood dripped from his ear canals.

"Report," Vekzara demanded.

Xylar didn't speak immediately. He stared at the construct on the viewscreen, now pulsing steadily with an ominous rhythm.

"It's not a weapon," he said finally. "It's a memory. And it's remembering us."

Xylar felt a cold weight settle behind his breastplate—not fear, but recognition. Something ancient stirred in his blood, echoing across generations bred for war but starved of memory. He wasn't prepared for this kind of enemy—not one carved from their forgotten past.

The bridge went silent.

Above Xylos, the structure flared—and then, without warning, dozens of similar signals ignited across the system.

The Swarm hadn't retreated.

They had made room.

For something far older.

For something that had finally... awakened.

Elsewhere on the command deck, officers scrambled to launch intercept protocols. The fleet AI stuttered as the system map filled with cascading red alerts.

"Command grid failing to isolate signal origins! They're jumping subspace layers faster than we can track."

"Initiate Grid Lockdown," Vekzara snapped.

"It failed," came the reply. "The grid didn't respond. It... mirrored us. Tactical feeds looping false positives. External commands are being issued—origin: us."

Vekzara slammed his clawed fist onto the console. "It's rewriting our war map."

Xylar's eyes narrowed. "They're not just coming. They're already here."

His voice dropped to a murmur, meant for no one but himself:

"And they remember everything we forgot."

Behind him, the orb pulsed once more.

Chapter 5: Devourer Rising

The fleet around Xylos spiraled into chaos. Warning alarms blared relentlessly through the command deck of the Razor's Kiss, punctuating the frenetic shouts of officers frantically attempting to stabilize a rapidly disintegrating tactical picture. Admiral Vekzara stood rigid, mandibles tightly clenched as he watched one outpost after another vanish silently from the holomap, devoured by cascading red markers.

"Grid sectors Omega-3 and Sigma-5 are dark," a tactical officer announced, her voice shaking slightly. "They're not destroyed—they're just...gone."

"Energy signatures?" Vekzara demanded.

"None," came the bewildered reply. "It's as if space itself opened and swallowed them."

Vekzara hesitated, mandibles clenching as he stared at the holomap. For a heartbeat, the flickering red markers bled into the outline of his failures—the ghosts of battles lost, lives wasted under his command. He had worn the mantle of leadership with pride, but now it felt like a shroud. A whisper of guilt threaded through his mind: "I should have seen this coming." Each red marker felt like a blade through his command, his mind racing through failed scenarios, unable to shake a creeping doubt. "Have I led us to ruin?" he wondered privately.

The smell of burned coolant and ionized air filled his nostrils. The tension on the deck was palpable, a living pressure pressing against his exoskeleton. He could feel the pulse of the artifact in storage, even through the reinforced bulkheads—a rhythm too deliberate, too aware.

Xylar entered the bridge, armor still scarred from the Echo's Claw mission, the haunted weight of the Memory Core's encounter evident in the stiffness of his shoulders. He scanned the scene, absorbing the panic before meeting Vekzara's hardened gaze.

"Admiral," Xylar said, voice grim, "we're running out of time."

Vekzara leaned into the table, mandibles twitching in suppressed rage. "The rogue faction believes these signals herald our ancient legacy. They've commandeered a dreadnought—The Relentless."

Xylar felt a chill course through him. "They're going after another artifact."

Vekzara nodded gravely. "On Illyris, the forgotten moon. Intelligence suggests it's tied to whatever these constructs are. Your team is to intercept, retrieve the artifact, and neutralize this rogue element."

Xylar hesitated only briefly, the memories of their last mission still fresh. But duty outweighed hesitation. "Understood, Admiral."

"And Xylar," Vekzara added sharply, "failure isn't an option. If Illyris falls, we lose everything."

The landing was silent, almost peaceful—a deceptive calm shrouding the jagged landscape of Illyris. Xylar and his squad, including Valerius, Gheda, Lorn, and the restless Rhalyx, fanned out from their dropship, weapons primed and senses strained.

The surface stretched out in an eerie twilight, blackened mountains clawing at an amber sky. The air was acrid, thick with a metallic tang that clung to the back of their throats. A low hum vibrated through the ground beneath their boots, like the dying breath of an ancient machine.

Every few paces, a sudden gust carried with it the scent of scorched minerals and something fouler—decay masked in ozone. Each step resonated through their armor as if disturbing ancient slumber. Faint keening winds echoed through rusted conduits, and the underfoot terrain hissed intermittently, exhaling gasps of warm, stagnant air that reeked of charred bone.

"Scanners up," Xylar ordered. "Keep formation tight."

Rhalyx's voice crackled nervously through the comm. "Reading scattered heat signatures ahead. Irregular patterns."

As they advanced, the terrain abruptly shifted, revealing twisted metal spires jutting upward, remnants of ancient Kryll architecture intertwined with something alien, pulsating like veins beneath a thin, membranous skin. The ground pulsed with warmth, and beneath the skin-like surface, faint lights moved in tandem with the squad's footsteps, as if responding.

Lorn stared in disgust. "It's alive."

Xylar knelt, running his gauntlet over the structure. His mind buzzed as though brushed by invisible tendrils. Whispers surged through his thoughts—haunted echoes of ancient Kryll dialects mixed with something utterly foreign.

Suddenly, a scream shattered the silence. A figure sprinted from the shadows—a rogue Kryll marine, armor corroded, eyes wild.

"It chose us!" he shrieked. "The Devourer has awakened!"

Before Xylar could respond, a swarm of twisted shapes surged behind the rogue marine. Creatures of shifting black alloys and twitching limbs, half-machine and half-organic nightmare—elongated skulls fused with pulsating circuitry, limbs that convulsed with erratic spasms, exuding a sickly stench of ozone and decay—surged toward them with grotesque speed. Some had faces stretched into permanent howls, others dragged their own entrails as offerings.

"Fire!" Xylar shouted.

Weapons erupted, plasma bolts tearing into the incoming constructs, sending sparks and viscera flying. The team formed a defensive perimeter, their fire disciplined but desperate as each wave grew thicker, more relentless.

Nearby, Gheda lunged forward, grabbing a fallen marine by the armor collar just before a construct's blade slammed into the ground. "Hold on!" she screamed, dragging him to safety amidst the chaos.

Gheda shouted over the chaos, "They're reanimating! Watch your fire!"

Horror crept through Xylar as fallen constructs twitched and rose again, pulling broken metal and discarded flesh into twisted new forms. The marines tightened their formation, driven into retreat, step by step.

A stray bolt slammed Lorn sideways, armor breached, pain flooding the comms. For a heartbeat, Xylar saw another battlefield, another marine lost under his command. The sting of old failures surged through him, raw and bitter. "Not again," he vowed silently. "Not here."

Rhalyx dragged Lorn back, snarling, firing one-handed into the thrashing mass.

In the distance, atop a ridge shrouded in ash-haze and flickering energy fields, the rogue Kryll sect had gathered. Cloaked in tattered crimson robes inscribed with cryptic runes, they chanted in low, rhythmic pulses—a haunting phrase that echoed across the valley: "Through silence, the Devourer speaks; through unity, we transcend." The very air around them shimmered with malignant energy, distorting light as if reality itself recoiled from their presence. Their chant deepened, overlapping in harmonic dissonance, sounding more like a summoning than any prayer.

"We need to reach them," Xylar ordered grimly, eyes narrowing. "Cut the head off this madness."

Through the maelstrom, they surged forward, fighting for every step. Valerius roared, breaking ranks to punch through a knot of constructs, his heavy gauntlets shattering enemy frames. Xylar followed, driven by desperation, pushing toward the cultists.

At the crest, the lead cultist turned, eyes glowing with an unnatural light. "Fools! The Devourer grants eternal life through unity. Your resistance only delays inevitable perfection."

Xylar lunged, energy blade extended, cutting down the nearest figure. The rest scattered in panic, their focus breaking the control of the constructs, which slowed and spasmed, confused.

Valerius grabbed the lead cultist, armor crackling with suppressed fury. "What have you done?"

The Kryll smiled, cold and empty. "We've opened the door."

Xylar turned to see the constructs begin vibrating, harmonics building into a deafening crescendo. The moon itself trembled.

"Fall back!" he ordered. "Extraction—now!"

They retreated, sprinting toward their waiting dropship, pursued by seismic eruptions and screaming constructs dissolving into clouds of living darkness. The cultist's laughter followed them, even as Valerius silenced him with a sharp strike.

Back aboard the Razor's Kiss, Vekzara stared gravely at the retrieved artifact—a gleaming sphere etched with Kryll runes, still pulsing faintly. For a moment, the pulse aligned with his own heartbeat, sending a chill down his spine. He couldn't shake the eerie sensation that it was watching him, mirroring him, like some cosmic echo testing the bounds of time. In the silence, the pulse quickened. Vekzara took an involuntary step back, memories from the last war against the Swarm flooding his mind like a cold tide.

A flicker of regret welled up in him—memories of past gambles, of unread signals dismissed as noise. Had he missed the signs again? He clenched a fist behind his back, hiding the tremble.

"It's identical to Memory Core 917," Xylar murmured. "If Memory Core 917 woke them up, maybe this one can shut them down. Or at least slow them."

Vekzara's eyes darkened. "Let's pray you're right. Because we're running out of options."

Xylar stared at the artifact, its surface shimmering faintly. Something ancient whispered again, resonating deep within him.

"The Devourer knows we're here," he said, voice heavy with grim certainty. "And it won't stop until it's consumed us all."

Behind them, the artifact pulsed once—bright, synchronized with the heartbeat of every being on the command deck.

And somewhere in the dark reaches of space... another pulse answered.

Chapter 6: Devourer War

Xylar stared at the galactic star map projected before him, the once-stable Kryll dominion now riddled with flares of hostile resonance. System after system flickered red—evidence of incursions, disturbances, or worse. Every echo traced back to the ancient signal. Every thread led to the Devourers.

The Razor's Kiss drifted in high orbit above Kryll Prime, her hull re-forged with null-void plating after the Illyris incursion. Inside, the war council chamber was cloaked in half-light, the only illumination coming from the tactical projection hovering between the attending officers. Xylar stood opposite Admiral Vekzara, and the silence between them was heavy, filled with unresolved tension and the weight of what they'd unleashed.

"They've struck Thalos," Vekzara said at last, voice grave. "No survivors. Our outposts are being overwritten, not just destroyed. Something is rewriting reality around these incursion points."

Xylar didn't blink. "We always thought the Swarm was the endgame. But they were just the veil. The Devourers are the storm."

Valerius stepped forward. "The artifact from Illyris is responding to Memory Core 917. It's emitting a low-frequency signal. Almost like it's... crying out."

"Or calling something," Vekzara muttered. "What do we know about the signal's pattern?"

"It resembles a resonance code," said Gheda, manipulating the hologram. "A sequence matching both Core signatures. It may be a trigger. Or a warning."

"Or both," Xylar added.

The room fell into tense silence.

Vekzara finally turned away from the projection. His mandibles clicked in rhythm, the sound betraying nerves he otherwise masked behind a hardened stare. In that flicker of silence, a thought crept through him like static—*What if I've already made the wrong call? What if bringing Xylar back set the entire stream on fire?* But his voice remained iron.

"We cannot afford hesitation. I've authorized a system-wide red alert. Evacuations of non-essential colonies begin immediately. Battle groups have been deployed to the Navoran belt and Helix Reach."

Valerius raised an eyebrow. "You think we can hold the line?"

Vekzara looked him dead in the eyes. "No. But we can buy time. Time for something better than blind resistance."

He turned to Xylar. "Your mission is now singular. Find out what these artifacts want. Where they came from. And whether we can use them before they use us."

The Echo's Claw descended into the irradiated belt surrounding the broken world of Tarsis-IV, a planet long-considered lost to ancient wars. The Core's signal had begun fluctuating, drifting toward coordinates that traced an impossible gravitational anomaly. Xylar and his team landed near a ruin half-swallowed by obsidian crystal growths.

"Looks like the planet's been growing tumors," Rhalyx muttered.

"That's not geological," Gheda replied, scanning the formations. "It's techno-organic. Resonant with the same frequencies as the artifacts."

The team advanced into the ruins, stepping carefully around collapsed archways and half-submerged chambers. The deeper they went, the more the ruins vibrated with a low hum, like a sleeping beast with shallow breath. A bitter, metallic scent thickened the air, and the faint crackling of energy made the walls hum against their armor.

In the core chamber, a massive construct dominated the room—a sphere three times the size of Core 917, suspended by anti-gravitic pylons. Its surface shimmered with a pattern that changed depending on where one looked, like it existed in more than one reality at once.

Xylar approached cautiously. "Memory Core 1019?"

A silence, and then a flicker.

"Designation correct," the sphere pulsed. "Observer unit located. Welcome, Echo bearer."

Valerius blinked. "It knows you."

The Core rippled again. "You carry resonance of the breach. You are a splinter of consequence."

Xylar stepped closer, frowning. "What do the Devourers want?"

"Devourers do not want. They correct. Realign. Preserve integrity of source stream."

"They think we're the infection," Gheda whispered.

"Incorrect," the Core countered. "You are fragmentation. Remnants of recursive failure. Your existence is unsanctioned deviation."

Rhalyx growled. "That's not much better."

Before they could ask more, the chamber trembled. Lights dimmed. Screams echoed through the ruins. Constructs burst from the shadows, twisted things with shifting geometry and mirrored faces—each reflecting the marines in grotesque distortion. Limbs clicked like metal on glass, bending in impossible angles, eyes like wet obsidian staring back with mirrored screams.

"Defensive posture!" Xylar barked.

The marines formed a ring, firing as the creatures charged. Valerius cut through one with a heavy blade, its form shattering into reflective shards that screamed before vanishing.

Gheda slammed a detonator against the chamber wall. "We have to leave!"

Xylar turned to the Core. "Is there a way to stop them?"

The Core shimmered. "Only reset. Memory overwrite. Reconnect to stream origin."

"What does that mean?!"

"You must descend. The Vault must be opened."

A new set of coordinates streamed into their visors.

"Fallback! Now!" Xylar shouted.

They raced for the surface, constructs swarming behind them. Explosions rocked the ruin as they lifted off, barely clearing the growths now surging upward, drawn by the Core's activation.

Back aboard the Razor's Kiss, Vekzara awaited their return. Xylar emerged from the dropship bloodied but alive.

"We have a path," he said. "A place called the Deep Vault. Buried on a dead moon. The Cores believe it holds the key."

Vekzara's expression tightened. He said nothing for a beat too long, eyes fixed on the blood drying along Xylar's armor. Then his jaw set.

"Then we're out of time. Prepare the fleet. We're going to open a wound history tried to forget."

And far beyond the system, in the void between stars, the Devourers shifted course. Drawn not by hatred—but by memory.

By correction.

By war.

And in the darkened containment vault aboard the Razor's Kiss, the first artifact pulsed—once, twice—then began to glow in rhythm with Xylar's heartbeat.

The echo had found its anchor.

Chapter 7: Shatterpoint

The war room aboard the Razor's Kiss had gone unnaturally quiet. Star maps flickered, systems chirped warnings, but all eyes stayed on the glowing sphere at the center of the table—Memory Core 1019, its surface pulsing with symbols none of them could translate fast enough. Xylar stood rigid before it, armor streaked with carbon scarring, blood dried in the seams.

Across the table, Admiral Vekzara's mandibles clicked in a slow rhythm, betraying the unrest he otherwise kept buried. A ghost of thought pressed against the back of his mind—*Illyris. The broken ridge. The marines I left behind.*

He was there again, if only in memory. The ridge had crumbled under plasma fire, its jagged edge glowing with molten hate. Screams cut through the static of his comms as his squad was overrun. He'd been ordered to pull back, to preserve command. But he'd seen their faces—Sawen, Revek, Illyris—fighting like hell even as the Swarm descended. And he'd left them. Not just left—abandoned. The last transmission had been a scream and the static hiss of a severed line.

He reached up and briefly touched the medallion buried beneath his battle cloak, the one awarded posthumously to a brother who never returned. He closed his eyes, just for a moment. The guilt hadn't faded—it had calcified, buried under cycles of duty. He reached up and briefly touched the medallion buried beneath his battle cloak, the one awarded posthumously to a brother who never returned. He closed his eyes, just for a moment. The guilt hadn't faded—it had calcified, buried under cycles of duty.

Valerius broke the silence. "What did the Core show you?"

Xylar's voice was low. "A vault. Buried in a dead moon. Not a prison—a seed vault. It called it the origin point. A fracture in time we were never supposed to survive."

Prime Core 1019 flickered and spun midair, shedding projections like shards of future possibilities. Its voice was layered with harmonics that sent a tremor through their bones.

"Time fractures with your every breath. Your existence is a ripple—an echo uncontained."

Valerius narrowed his eyes. "What does that even mean?"

Prime Core rotated again. "Your war is recursive. The Devourers correct deviation. The Vault must be reached. Or all streams collapse."

Vekzara stepped forward, bracing both hands on the table. "How do we stop them?"

Prime Core pulsed with a burst of light—and suddenly, every marine saw something different.

Valerius saw the battlefield of Thalos drenched in violet flame. Gheda saw herself standing alone in a corridor of mirrors, unable to find her face. Rhalyx saw a youngling version of himself, absorbed into a swarm of humming black.

And Xylar—he saw the ghost of Illyris. The mountain shattered. The eyes of the dying marine who begged him not to leave.

He staggered back.

Prime Core's voice echoed again: "To reach origin is to unmake self. One must remember what was never permitted."

Alarms flared suddenly—proximity warnings.

"Vessel inbound!" cried a sensor officer. "Non-Kryll signature. Massive. It just blinked into our plane!"

The Devourer ship appeared on the edge of the system, dark as obsidian and shaped like a broken blade.

Vekzara's calm snapped. "Shields up! Ready all batteries!"

He looked at Xylar. "Get to that Vault. If we fall, make sure it wasn't for nothing."

Xylar nodded. "You'll hold the line?"

The admiral paused, eyes heavy. "No. But I'll delay the inevitable. That's enough."

He turned away from the hologrid, and in that fleeting moment of solitude, the admiral whispered to no one, "Forgive me, Illyris. I still don't know if I was wrong."

The Echo's Claw dove through void currents toward the abandoned moon of Caerun. Its surface was cracked and scorched from old plasma burns. Beneath that skin—according to the Core—lay the Vault.

"No life signs," Gheda reported. "But there's something under the crust. It's humming."

They disembarked into a blackened crater, following tunnels carved by something not mechanical. The air was stale, sharp with iron, and the floor vibrated faintly with each breath. An unnatural hum threaded through the silence, like metal breathing. The distant sound of dripping echoed somewhere beyond, too rhythmic to be water, and the shadows bent just slightly wrong—like they remembered movement that hadn't yet happened. The scent of ionized decay lingered—like blood mixed with ash.

Deeper still, they found it: a vault door grown into the stone itself, etched with the same symbols seen across all the Cores. As they approached, a series of low, guttural chants echoed from within the rock.

Rhalyx froze. "That's not natural."

Valerius listened, then frowned. "They're speaking in harmonic code. A phrase repeated: 'Only the unmade remember. Let the silence dream.' The phrase resonated through the chamber like a sacred echo—a mantra from the shadows of Kryll mythos. Among the oldest cult texts, it symbolized surrender to memory's dissolution, the belief that forgetting was defiance, but remembering was obedience. In this place, it wasn't just eerie—it was prophecy."

Xylar stepped forward. His heartbeat thudded in his ears—and beneath that, he felt the Core's pulse syncing with it. Like a second heart.

"What do we do?" Gheda asked.

He placed his hand on the door.

"We open it."

The door split in perfect silence.

Inside, a chamber of swirling resonance stretched into darkness. Floating within—hundreds of crystalline minds, shards of past Cores, each reflecting memories not their own. In the center: a pedestal. And on it, a shape.

A humanoid figure made of refracted metal and light.

Its head lifted.

And it spoke.

"Welcome home, Echo."

Then, everything trembled.

The cultists—no longer whispers in the wall—emerged from the shadows. Grotesque figures, fused with machine and time, their forms flickering at the edges as if partially out of phase. Metallic tendrils writhed beneath translucent skin, their faces half-formed and twitching as if reshaped by memory alone. The air around them rippled with an oily shimmer, carrying a stench of scorched circuitry and rotting code. Their joints cracked with each step, emitting discordant chimes like broken instruments, and their eyes—if they could be called that—glowed with the cold fire of forgotten timelines. Their skin was an ever-shifting lattice of circuitry and flesh, veins glowing with quantum bleed.

They chanted louder now: "Unmake the wound. Restore the stream. Let the silence dream."

One of them lunged. Xylar dodged, firing point-blank. The creature exploded in shards that crawled toward the pedestal, reforming like liquid metal seeking shape.

"We have to shut it down!" Gheda screamed.

"No," Xylar said, locking eyes with the Echo figure. "We have to listen."

The figure raised a hand. From its palm, a projection flared—stars folding, timelines rippling like cloth. A cosmic lattice beyond comprehension. And in its heart, the Devourers.

Not destroyers.

Custodians.

Rhalyx's voice cracked. "Then who are the real invaders?"

The vault walls pulsed in rhythm with the artifact in Xylar's chest. It glowed brighter—matching his breath. His heartbeat. Then... something else.

The figure looked to Xylar one last time.

It tilted its head—just as he had days ago before the Prime Core. A gesture of recognition. Of mirroring.

"You already know."

Then it shattered.

The pedestal cracked.

And the Core in Xylar's chest began to scream—its pulse thundering in perfect sync with his heartbeat. Xylar staggered, hand instinctively clutching at his chest, as if the artifact had become a living thing inside him. A rush of memory surged through his mind—Illyris's final gaze, the unending war, the Vault's silent promise—and with it, the unbearable weight of realization. This wasn't destiny. It was reckoning.

In the containment bay far above, the first artifact exploded into radiant light.

And across Kryll space, the Cores awakened.

Aboard the Razor's Kiss, Vekzara stood on the command deck as the Devourer ship began to move.

One officer whispered, "They're not targeting us. The y're... waiting."

Vekzara didn't move.

His gaze fixed on the horizon, on a war no longer his to understand. The whisper of guilt returned. The memory of voices lost beneath foreign stars.

And deep inside him, a long-buried fear stirred awake—*What if we were never the heroes?*

Chapter 8: The Unraveling Silence

The Echo's Claw moved through space like a blade through silk, descending toward the fractured moon of Caerun. Below, the Vault's signal pulsed louder with each passing second. Within the ship, Xylar stood at the viewport, his reflection caught between stars and shadow. The Core embedded in his chest glowed softly—responding. The silence outside was deceptive; something ancient stirred beneath the surface.

Gheda's voice crackled over the comm. "Approach vector confirmed. No hostile signatures, but the resonance... it's growing."

Xylar didn't answer immediately. His hand drifted to his chest, fingers tracing the heat radiating from the Core. It beat with his pulse now. It felt alive—almost sentient. The glow pulsed in rhythm with the Vault below, as though it called to him in a forgotten language.

Vekzara's voice came through next, taut with tension. "Xylar, the Razor's Kiss will maintain orbit, but we can't stay long. If the Devourers move again—"

"Understood," Xylar cut in. "If we fail, you'll know."

Moments later, they landed. The moon's crust crackled beneath their boots as the away team moved out. Rhalyx led with his blade staff ignited, Valerius scanned their perimeter, and Gheda adjusted a portable relay to maintain their link to the ship. Dust floated in the low gravity, catching the faint glow of distant stars.

Beneath the moon's surface, the tunnels narrowed. Etchings lit as they passed, symbols shifting in their peripheral vision. The walls seemed to breathe. Whispers, barely audible, threaded through the stone like veins of sound. The air thinned, whispering memories.

"The Vault's deeper," Valerius muttered. "We're being led."

"Not led," Rhalyx said, voice low. "Judged."

A silence settled, broken only by the rhythmic hum that echoed with their steps. It wasn't just sound—it was a feeling in their bones, like being watched by something older than memory.

They entered the chamber.

A cathedral of light and memory, wider than any sensor had predicted. Crystalline shards floated midair, rotating like relics in prayer. Every motion left behind a trail of lingering sound, like echoes folded through time. The smell of scorched ozone mixed with the strange sweetness of alien minerals. In the center stood the Echo—the refracted humanoid figure of light and metal. It turned as they entered, gaze settling on Xylar.

"The cycle breaks," it said. "Echo returns."

Xylar stepped forward. "What am I?"

The Echo raised an arm. Projections bloomed—time shattered into cascading lattices, scenes folding over each other. A battleground of black stars. The fall of Caerun. The betrayal. The Core in Xylar's chest began to pulse harder, syncing with the vision.

"You are the fracture born of resistance. The wound that learned to feel."

He remembered the silence of command halls, the cold echo of unsanctioned decisions. The memory wasn't his—but it had been seeded into him, threaded with every pulse of the Core. Was he still Kryll, or something else rising from their ashes?

Suddenly, the chamber rippled. Chanting rose—"Let the silence dream." From the edges, the cultists emerged, their robes like ash trailing through time. Eyes aglow with harmonic fire, they stepped forward in synchronization.

But something was different.

Xylar didn't raise his weapon. Instead, he stepped closer to the Echo. The light engulfed him—and he saw.

Caerun had once been a Kryll colony, razed not by the Devourers, but by their own command, fearing contamination from what the Vault held. He saw flashes of Council deliberations, the fear in Vekzara's younger eyes as he gave the order to sterilize the moon. Behind him, other commanders averted their gaze, silent not in agreement, but in fear.

"Containment exceeds tolerance," Vekzara's younger voice echoed in the vision. "The Vault must not awaken."

The Devourers hadn't arrived to destroy—they had come to preserve a balance the Kryll had shattered.

Xylar turned. The cultists had stopped advancing.

"They remember," the Echo said. "Fragments. Echoes. They are memory incarnate."

One cultist reached toward Xylar—not in violence, but reverence. Its face flickered between past and present. A former marine. Illyris.

Illyris had died years ago—devoured during the Scour Rift campaign. But here she stood, face shimmering between then and now. Had the Vault pulled her soul from the fracture? Or had memory become flesh?

Xylar gasped, knees buckling. The guilt he'd buried ruptured in his chest. He staggered forward, clutching the Core. It screamed again, vibrating with grief and revelation. The weight of Caerun's ashes pulled at him like gravity.

The Echo placed a hand on his shoulder.

"Let the wound breathe. Let the stream choose."

Everything convulsed. The chamber imploded inward, warping around them. Time and space twisted, folding in on itself like origami dipped in fire. The Core in Xylar's chest pulsed in sync with his heartbeat—no longer just a relic, but a conscience. A choice.

Aboard the Razor's Kiss, Vekzara watched as the Vault erupted in a spiraling vortex of energy. He gripped the rail, eyes wide. This wasn't destruction—it was rebirth. The Devourer ship remained still, as if bowing. The stars around it flickered, distorted by the resonance field now spreading from Caerun.

"Sir... the Cores... across the system. They're activating," a comms officer reported, panic behind her voice.

Vekzara said nothing. Only stared into the unraveling light. His fingers curled, knuckles whitening. This had begun long ago, with an order he couldn't undo.

A voice—not from the ship, not from any comm—whispered into his mind.

You have unmade the silence.

On the monitor, the Devourers turned away. A gesture of acknowledgment—or of finality.

And Kryll history began to rewrite itself.

Far beyond the stars, something else stirred—watching the unraveling silence, waiting for the stream to break.

Chapter 9: Faultlines of the Deep

Darkness was no longer a void—it was a presence.

The *Crimson Corsair* moved in low orbit above Nevaris, the third moon of Ephyra Prime. Jagged ridgelines of black obsidian fractured the horizon below, glowing faintly with subterranean pulses. Seismic activity registered in steady tremors, but what stirred below wasn't tectonic.

It was something else.

Xylar stood on the bridge, watching the shifting crust with narrowed eyes. His Core pulsed faintly, responding to harmonic frequencies no one else could hear. He'd barely spoken since the Vault.

Rhalyx leaned over the console beside him. "The deeper scans aren't bouncing back anymore. We're getting echoes, but no walls. It's like the rock below is hollow—alive."

Gheda swore under her breath. "Another Vault?"

"No," Xylar said, his voice low. "A fracture. The Echo unlocked more than memory. It shifted something beneath the surface of all this."

Vekzara appeared on the hololink, his image ghostly with static. "Preliminary reports from other Core sites confirm activation. Whatever you triggered on Caerun is spreading. Entire planetary crusts are destabilizing. Our analysts suspect the Vaults were suppressing deeper phenomena."

Xylar didn't flinch. "And now we've set them free."

Below, a series of obsidian ridges split open in a sudden bloom of red mist and shrieking resonance. The tremor rocked the ship. Sirens wailed.

"Gravitic flux!" Gheda yelled. "Something's pulling at the Corsair's core! Reversing polarity!"

Xylar gripped the console. The Core in his chest beat harder.

"We go down," he said.

"Are you insane?" Rhalyx snapped. "We don't even know what's alive down there."

"That's the point," Xylar said. "Whatever's awakening ... it remembers me."

The descent shuttle pierced the clouds like a falling spear. Storms laced with crimson lightning danced across the upper atmosphere. Below, the terrain shimmered and twisted, as if the laws of physics faltered under the resonance field. The scent of ozone and scorched metal filled the cabin.

They landed hard against the ridge, the impact reverberating through their armor.

Xylar led the way with Rhalyx and Gheda behind him. Valerius remained aboard the shuttle, monitoring from above.

They entered the fracture.

Obsidian walls spiraled inward, not carved but grown—formed by pressure and memory. The path beneath their feet responded to their movement, glowing faintly in Kryll script that shimmered and then vanished. The temperature dropped with each step, the air thickening with a coppery tang. Faint vibrations played beneath their skin like forgotten melodies. A distant hum filled the air, like a choir singing a dirge from beneath the ground.

"This was made by us," Rhalyx whispered. "But not any Kryll still living."

As they descended, the walls began to pulse with low, harmonic tones—subsonic vibrations that played across their bones. Xylar flinched as one tone matched the rhythm of his Core.

They passed remnants of ancient armor, broken helms fused with the walls, bone etched with chanting runes. A sense of mourning soaked the stone. Gheda reached out, brushing a fragment with her fingers. "These weren't buried. They were offered."

Xylar paused. One of the runes caught his eye—"Esh'varun"—the Forgotten Song. A lament said to summon the echoes of the fallen. His chest tightened.

At the chasm's core, they found it: a massive chamber encasing a sphere of suspended crystal and bone. Within it floated the shape of something humanoid, but impossibly old. Its body was partially encased in armor, but the face was unmistakable—a Kryll warrior-priest of the First Generation.

Gheda gasped. "Is that..."

"The Prime Seer," Xylar said. "One of the first to bind with a Core."

Xylar stepped closer, his gaze drawn to the fine cracks in the crystal, as if time itself had tried to break in but failed. A dull vibration resonated through his feet, growing stronger the nearer he came.

Suddenly, the sphere pulsed. A voice—not heard, but felt—reverberated in their minds.

Echoes awaken. The Silence bleeds. We are the hymn before the rupture.

The air cracked with resonance. Xylar staggered, clutching his Core. It responded violently, flashing brighter than ever before.

Rhalyx dropped to one knee, gasping. "It's... rewriting something."

A memory—his own—flashed through Xylar's mind unbidden: a younger version of himself, kneeling in a collapsed temple, surrounded by bodies, Core fragments buried in their chests. The same hum echoed then. The same dread. His hands had trembled as he lifted the last dying priest, whispering apologies. The silence that followed had never left him.

The Prime Seer's eyes opened.

They glowed with harmonic fire.

You have fractured the stream.

Above, aboard the *Crimson Corsair*, Valerius watched from orbit. His sensors began picking up movement across Nevaris.

From the fault lines emerged humanoid shapes of obsidian and bone. Not machines. Not alive. Echoes of war.

Armored, weaponized, and pulsing with the same energy signature as the Core in Xylar's chest.

He opened a comm.

"Captain, we've got company. Lots of it. Something's calling to them."

In the chamber below, the Prime Seer began to lift a hand, slow and ceremonial, as the chamber darkened. The harmonic light now pulsed like a heartbeat—synchronized with Xylar's Core. The sound in the chamber took on rhythm, like the distant toll of a cracked bell.

The fracture will complete the hymn. The silence must break fully. Or all will drown in resonance.

A sudden screech reverberated from the tunnel behind them. One of the obsidian figures had entered, followed by dozens more. Their eyes burned with identical fire. But they didn't attack.

They knelt.

"To you," Rhalyx whispered, disbelief coating every word.

Xylar turned to the others. "This wasn't just a memory. This is a directive."

Gheda stepped forward, her weapon still trained on the figures. "A directive from what? Some remnant of the past?"

"No," Xylar said. "From the future. One that remembers us failing."

The Prime Seer reached out a hand. A shard of crystal detached from the sphere, hovering in front of Xylar's chest. His Core pulsed, drawing it in.

Complete the hymn, the Seer intoned. *Only the fracture leads to resonance reborn.*

A jolt ran through Xylar's body as the shard embedded itself into his Core. His vision blurred.

He saw cities burning—not human, not Kryll, something else—flames licking at towers made of songstone and memory. He saw a sky torn open, harmonic frequencies screaming across worlds. He saw his own hands stained with energy, choosing who lived... and who didn't.

He gasped.

And the chamber echoed with the sound of it—like a broken note lingering at the end of a forgotten melody.

Chapter 10: Harmonic Siege

The sky above Nevaris wept ash.

Aboard the *Crimson Corsair*, Valerius watched in grim silence as hundreds of figures emerged from the cracked ridges below. Their forms glistened with obsidian armor, joints laced with bone, and each movement echoed a forgotten discipline. They weren't erratic. They were marching.

"Estimate?" he asked.

The tactical AI replied in a low hum. "Three thousand and rising. Patterned formation. Resonant synchronization detected."

Valerius's fingers danced across the console. He opened a secure channel. "Bridge to Commander Xylar. We have a problem topside."

Static.

Then a whisper: "They follow him."

Below the surface, Xylar's mind reeled. The shard embedded in his Core thrummed with violent harmony, each beat pulling at threads of memory, prophecy, and something deeper—will. The Prime Seer's presence faded into the crystal as if its task had been completed, the sphere dimming until it resembled a relic long dead.

"We need to move," Rhalyx said, scanning the kneeling figures. "This place feels like it's holding its breath."

Xylar looked down at his hands. They trembled faintly.

You have been chosen.

He didn't know if the voice was still the Seer's or something new, but its weight settled like a commandment.

The obsidian warriors parted as the Kryll passed through. They remained motionless, save for the subtle hum that passed from one to the next. Gheda kept her weapon raised.

"You really think they're... on our side?"

Xylar answered without looking back. "I think they remember who I was."

The surface greeted them with chaos.

Atmospheric resonance had destabilized the magnetic poles. Storms surged like wild serpents across the sky, bleeding aurorae in colors never cataloged. The shuttle was gone—or rather, scattered in molten fragments along the ridge.

"Valerius!" Xylar barked into the comm. "Report!"

The line crackled.

"Corsair is compromised. Auto-defenses engaged. Something hit us from orbit—a harmonic spike. It wasn't natural."

Rhalyx looked skyward. A ripple of violet fire expanded in a slow spiral above them.

"What the hell is that?"

Gheda's expression hardened. "It's a beacon. Someone wants everyone to know what just woke up."

Above the moon, beyond the thin veil of Nevaris's exosphere, another ship lurked.

It wasn't Kryll. And it wasn't human.

The *Ossuary Dawn* bore no emblem, no allegiance. A vessel of bone-fused metal, it pulsed with a resonance of its own, almost predatory. Inside, the figures were eyeless, draped in flesh-coded robes. Each carried a staff tipped with shattered Core fragments. At the center, a being known only as the Choirmaster stood before a suspended orb of red light.

"The fracture has begun," it murmured. "And the hymn approaches dissonance."

A voice replied from the orb, layered with broken harmonics: "Then silence them."

Xylar, Rhalyx, and Gheda raced through a canyon as harmonic blasts rained from the sky, carving obsidian into molten rivers.

A column of the kneeling warriors followed behind them, silently mirroring their path. One fell, shattered by a resonance burst—only to disintegrate into motes of light and memory, which rejoined the Core embedded in Xylar's chest.

He staggered but kept going.

Gheda grabbed his arm. "You didn't absorb it. It offered itself. What the hell are you becoming?"

Xylar didn't answer. He couldn't.

His mind was too full of voices. Old ones. Future ones. Ones that sounded like his own.

Valerius rerouted power from the Corsair's damaged engines to weapon systems. He targeted the shape breaking from the clouds above—a spire-shaped projectile, too fast and too quiet.

"Incoming strike! All decks brace!"

The *Corsair* was hit. Not with explosives, but with a pulse.

Everything stopped.

AI systems froze. Lights dimmed. Crew members dropped to their knees, clutching their skulls as dissonant harmonics poured through their senses like molten glass.

Valerius alone remained standing, eyes wide.

He was immune.

Or worse—expected.

A voice crawled through the bridge.

"Echo-bearer detected. You stand upon the threshold. Choose: song or silence."

Back on the ground, Xylar fell to his knees.

The shard in his Core flared, and a wave of force burst from his body, knocking back the warriors behind him. Rhalyx and Gheda braced themselves but remained standing.

Xylar gasped. The vision returned:

A choir of broken beings, howling across time. A gateway of resonance, half-open. A world on the other side screaming in pitch-perfect horror.

Complete the hymn.

He rose.

"We need to get to the convergence point," he said.

Gheda frowned. "There's no map. No data."

Xylar pointed east. "I don't need a map. I can hear it."

In the sky above Nevaris, the *Ossuary Dawn* turned, its prow glowing with malignant harmony. The Choirmaster raised his staff.

"Send the Dissonants."

Below, on the fractured world, echoes of bone and fury began to move again—no longer kneeling.

They were singing.

And their hymn was war.

Chapter 11: The Resonant Divide

The fractured plains of Nevaris groaned beneath a red-streaked sky, as if the moon itself were trying to scream. The seismic tremors no longer pulsed randomly—they were rhythmic. Intentional. Each beat matched the cadence of something stirring in the deep.

Xylar led the vanguard along the obsidian ridge, his movements guided less by logic and more by instinct—or something masquerading as it. Behind him, Rhalyx, Gheda, and a dwindling column of harmonic warriors followed, their silent formation eerie against the chaos.

Ahead, the terrain had changed. Crystalline spires erupted from the ground, humming in low tones that vibrated in the marrow. Air shimmered, thick with resonance.

"We're near the convergence," Xylar said, voice hollow.

Rhalyx looked at him, sweat streaking through the dust on his face. "Are we walking into a trap?"

"Maybe. Or maybe we're the fuse."

Gheda knelt near one of the crystalline formations. "These aren't natural. They're amplifiers. Something's preparing to transmit."

A sudden shockwave knocked them all to the ground. The sky cracked with a howl of frequencies never meant for ears. Xylar clutched his chest as the Core embedded there flared bright enough to illuminate the canyon. The harmonic warriors fell to one knee in unison, as if in reverence—or submission.

Above, the Crimson Corsair limped through the atmosphere, its hull scorched and systems stuttering. On the bridge, Valerius gripped the command rail as the Choirmaster's dissonant signal flooded the sensors. The AI core flickered, speaking in broken tongues.

"Entity approaching. Interference level critical. Identity... mirrored."

Valerius stared at the feed—a second Xylar, or something like him, walking through the storm toward the convergence point. Only this one was fused with bone, his Core blackened and pulsing erratically. His gait was familiar, but the aura was alien.

A line of data blinked across the screen: Subject resonance: inverse polarity.

"Begin planetary broadcast," Valerius ordered. "Everyone still breathing needs to see this."

Down in the canyon, Xylar gasped as a sudden vision seized him.

He stood not on Nevaris, but in a mirrored version of it. The same ridges, the same fracture—but draped in shadow. In this place, the Dissonants ruled. He saw himself—or a version of himself—leading them.

The Prime Seer stood beside this shadow-Xylar, hand outstretched.

One path leads to resonance. The other to annihilation. Which will you sing?

The Seer's voice faded, but a flicker of memory returned—Xylar on a battlefield as a young commander, choosing strategy over mercy. That echo now mirrored the cruelty of the corrupted self.

He snapped back to reality with a cry, and Gheda caught his arm.

"What did you see?"

He shook his head. "A warning. And a choice. One I've made before."

A new sound reached them—a collective hum, growing louder by the second. Over the next ridge, a wall of Dissonants approached. Not running. Marching. As if summoned.

Rhalyx readied his weapon. "We stand or we fall."

Xylar raised his hand. "No. We resonate."

He stepped forward. The harmonic warriors behind him responded, rising in unison. Xylar lifted his arms, and the Core inside him sang.

The note split the air like lightning.

The canyon responded.

The crystalline spires lit up, sending waves of harmonic energy crashing into the advancing Dissonants. The lead ranks faltered, disintegrating into ash and echo. But the ones behind kept coming, voices rising in chaotic dissonance.

The two waves collided—harmony against entropy.

In the skies, the Ossuary Dawn lowered its prow.

The Choirmaster whispered to the orb. "The hymn fractures. Send the twins."

Two figures emerged from the shadows of the ship. Not Kryll. Not machine. Something in between. Bound by shared resonance, their steps synchronized.

Twins. Mirrors.

As they moved, one whispered in tones only the other understood: "Sing it clean."

The second responded, voice like scraping bone, "Or sing it dead."

They descended.

Valerius watched it unfold from the Corsair's broken bridge. He transmitted Xylar's last known coordinates across all frequencies.

"This is our line. If we lose here, we lose the stream."

The crew, battered and disoriented, rallied. Power rerouted to ground support. Weapons recharged.

Below, the battlefield ignited.

Xylar fought like a man possessed. His Core surged with each blow, and the harmonic warriors responded to his movement like a living song. Rhalyx covered his flank, Gheda directing the energy flows from the crystalline nodes to buy time.

Then the Twins landed.

The impact cratered the ridge. One moved with speed, the other with overwhelming force. Together, they embodied dissonance incarnate.

The first came at Xylar.

Their blades met—a shattering sound of feedback and light. Xylar staggered back as his Core pulsed out of rhythm. The second Twin moved toward Gheda, who fired a harmonic blast that barely slowed it.

Rhalyx tackled the creature, dragging it into one of the crystalline nodes, triggering a detonation that flung them both clear. As he lay dazed, a single thought echoed in his mind—This was the vision.

Xylar screamed, turning his Core inward, forcing it to synchronize. A shockwave burst outward, catching the first Twin mid-strike and throwing it into a wall of glassy obsidian.

The Choirmaster watched it all.

"Let the hymn end... or let it consume."

But the song wasn't over.

Xylar stood, bleeding, breath ragged.

"As long as I resonate, the hymn survives."

And the ground itself answered.

One of the Dissonants faltered, falling to its knees—not in defeat, but in conflict. It looked to Xylar, then to the Twins, and back again.

A flicker of choice.

The battle had not just cracked the earth.

It had fractured allegiance.

Chapter 12: Harmonic Fall

Ash and obsidian rained from the fractured skies of Nevaris. The battlefield below shimmered with the aftershocks of harmonic warfare. Crystalline spires cracked, dissonant energies colliding with resonant force as the Kryll warriors fought to hold their ground. The convergence had begun—there was no turning back.

Xylar staggered through the wreckage, his Core flickering with unstable light. Every beat pulsed pain through his chest. His duel with the first Twin had left internal fractures—physical and otherwise.

He caught a glimpse of the second Twin across the ridge, bearing down on Gheda again. She hurled harmonic bursts to deflect it, but her energy was fading. The crystalline nodes she channeled were dimming—burning out from overload.

"We can't keep this up," Rhalyx growled, limping toward Xylar. Blood streaked his temple, but he still carried his resonance rifle, still fought like a cornered beast.

Xylar didn't answer. He could feel something under the surface. A pull. A call. Not the enemy's, not the Core's—but something older.

"There," he said, pointing to a broken fissure in the ridge. Harmonic script pulsed faintly beneath the rubble.

Rhalyx followed his gaze. "Another vault?"

"No. A memory. Buried in the stone."

They reached it just as the second Twin launched a projectile that shattered the ledge above them. Debris rained down. Xylar shielded Rhalyx with a barrier of pure resonance. It strained his Core nearly to rupture.

Gheda reached them. Her face was pale, lips trembling from Core overuse. "The Twins are gaining sync. If they merge harmonics—"

"—we die," Rhalyx finished grimly.

Xylar knelt before the fissure. His hand trembled as he touched the glyphs. They flared to life, revealing a spiraling chamber below. A resonance not of memory, but prophecy, thrummed beneath.

He turned to the others. "This is where the song changes."

They descended.

The chamber was unlike the others. Instead of vault stone or organic lattice, it was shaped from harmonic glass—each wall reflecting a possible future. Some showed victory. Others... decay. One image caught Xylar's eye: a world devoured by harmonic entropy, where nothing remained but the song's static echo.

In the center, a platform rose. Upon it, a fragment: not a Core, but something adjacent. A bridge of frequency. A tuner.

Gheda's eyes widened. "That's a Phase Chime. They were only theorized—tools to anchor resonance across divergent timelines."

Xylar nodded. "We're out of sync. We have to realign."

He stepped onto the platform. The Chime pulsed. Instantly, visions assaulted him.

—A younger version of himself walking away from a dying mentor.

—The Prime Seer weeping beside a shattered Core.

—The Choirmaster offering a choice: power or unity.

His Core screamed under the strain, resonance wavering. Another flicker came—a future where the Kryll fractured beyond repair, and his name became a curse.

The Twins appeared at the chamber's edge.

"You are fractured," one said.

"You are unfinished," said the other.

"But you can be rewritten," they said together.

They advanced. Gheda threw up a barrier, but the Twins began harmonizing their frequencies, building to a crescendo.

Xylar focused. He tuned into the Phase Chime, letting go of his fear. Instead of resisting, he opened his Core.

A harmonic pulse surged outward. The chamber shifted, glass becoming light. The visions aligned—not one future, but one truth.

Xylar's voice echoed with layered tones. "I am not fractured. I am the bridge."

The harmonic blast shattered the Twins' synchronization. One was thrown back. The other staggered, eyes flickering with uncertainty.

Above, the Crimson Corsair locked onto the signal. Valerius ordered an orbital drop of a harmonic amplifier—a last resort.

"Send it," he said. "If Xylar fails, this might turn the tide."

The amplifier plummeted, trailing fire.

In the chamber, the second Twin lunged at Gheda. Rhalyx intercepted, driving a vibro-blade into the joint of its shoulder. Sparks flew. The Twin shrieked.

Xylar stepped off the platform. The Phase Chime remained glowing, synchronized to him.

He raised his hand.

The amplifier struck outside, sending a shockwave of resonance through the ground. Channeled through the Chime, it became a song—a true harmonic alignment.

The Twins screamed. One collapsed into dust. The other blinked—then fell to its knees.

"I... remember," it whispered.

Xylar approached slowly. "Then choose. Join us—or fade."

The surviving Twin looked at its trembling hands. Then nodded.

A silence followed—dense and reverent.

Valerius' voice crackled over comms. "Report."

Xylar exhaled. "We held the stream."

Outside, the dissonance receded. The crystalline spires dimmed.

But far above, aboard the Ossuary Dawn, the Choirmaster simply turned and whispered to the shadows behind him.

"Let the Architects begin their verse."

Chapter 13: The Shattered Verse

The battlefield above Nevaris smoldered with the scent of ionized dust and the last chords of a fractured hymn. Silence spread unnaturally across the scorched ridge—an eerie calm after the crescendo of battle.

Xylar stood at the chamber's mouth, eyes locked on the kneeling Twin who had chosen not to strike. The harmonic glow from the Phase Chime behind them pulsed with faint regularity, like a dying heartbeat made steady again. But the resonance hadn't stilled; it had merely quieted to listen.

"Why do I still feel it?" Gheda whispered. She leaned against the chamber wall, her fingers trembling as she traced the harmonic glyphs etched into the glass-like surface. "The song changed... but something else is singing back."

Xylar turned to her. "Because the war isn't over. This was only the verse before the fall."

The Twin looked up, voice subdued, almost human. "We were created to fracture the stream. But some fragments remember the harmony. I remember... a voice. Someone who used to sing to us. Before the Cryo-vats. Before the pain."

Before Xylar could respond, the commlink on his wrist sparked to life. Valerius' voice filtered through the static. "We've intercepted a new broadcast—origin unknown. Multiple signatures. You're not alone down there."

Gheda straightened. "Another faction?"

"Not Kryll," Valerius said. "And not Dissonant either. These signals... they're ancient."

A shudder ran through the chamber. One of the harmonic glass walls rippled, distorting an image of a Kryll city—not in ruin, but untouched, suspended in time. The next pane showed the same city crumbling beneath tidal waves of dissonance. Another fragment briefly showed Gheda as Choirmaster, weeping alone in a fortress of glass.

A fourth showed Rhalyx, standing atop a mountain of Kryll dead, wearing Xylar's Core.

Rhalyx stepped forward, flanked by two surviving harmonic warriors. "What are we looking at?"

Gheda stared at the flickering walls. "Temporal reflections. Futures trying to assert themselves. If one wins... we lose choice."

The Phase Chime pulsed again, but erratically.

The surviving Twin blinked slowly. "The Chime is becoming unstable. It was never meant to be used by one alone."

Xylar stepped forward. "You said you remembered. Then prove it. Stand with me. We'll attune it together. Anchor the stream, or watch it collapse."

The Twin hesitated. Then, silently, stepped onto the platform beside him.

The moment their cores aligned, the chamber erupted in light. Time fractured.

They stood in a shattered field of possibilities—an endless hall of mirrored versions of themselves. In one shard, Xylar led an empire of resonance. In another, he was hunted by the remnants of the Kryll. In a third, nothing existed but the dissonance. In a fourth, Gheda's face stared at him coldly from a throne of glass.

He turned to the Twin. "Show me what you were."

The Twin's reflection changed: once a warrior of the Choir, then a child in a cryo-vat, then a conduit for the Choirmaster's failed experiments. One version wept beside another who killed without thought.

"We were meant to erase the harmonic stream. But our resonance... it was never complete. Not without belief. Not without choice."

Xylar extended a hand. "Then let's complete it. Together."

They reemerged in the chamber, the Phase Chime stabilizing. New glyphs emerged—ones no Kryll had seen in centuries. A soft note played—not from the Chime, but from the walls themselves. A faded melody that hadn't been heard in eons drifted across the chamber, haunting and unresolved.

Gheda gasped. "Those aren't harmonic runes. They're pre-Prime Seer script."

Rhalyx stepped closer. "Ancient architecture. Before the Choir. Before the Stream. This was the original verse."

Suddenly, the walls shook. A scream not of voice but of memory flooded the space. The chamber shimmered, then ruptured into a long-forgotten vault. Dust fell from vaulted ceilings etched in spiral glyphs. The Chime had opened a gate—to something older.

Valerius' voice returned. "Multiple anomalies across the planet. It's like Nevaris is waking up."

Xylar steadied himself. "Not waking up. Recalling. This planet's history was rewritten. We're seeing the first version. The unedited song."

Gheda stepped into the new chamber. "Then the Choirmaster didn't just want control of the stream. He wanted to overwrite the root composition."

The Twin followed, uncertain. "And now that we've opened this... he'll come. To finish the rewrite. To erase the original harmony."

A slow sound echoed behind them—metal dragging across crystal.

They turned.

From the far end of the vault, the Choirmaster stepped into view. But it wasn't just him. He moved like a conductor among shadows. And behind him... were others. Figures cloaked in fractured light, their forms flickering between dimensions. A glyph above the vault pulsed faintly—an eight-point lattice slowly unraveling.

"The Architects," Gheda said, breath catching. "They're real."

The Choirmaster's voice resonated without speaking. "You've touched the first verse. How quaint. Shall we begin the final movement?"

Xylar and the Twin stepped forward. The Phase Chime flared between them.

"Not unless you can match the harmony," Xylar replied.

Behind him, Rhalyx, Gheda, and the harmonic warriors fell into formation. The chamber hummed—not with fear, but with unity. Above them, the glyph lattice ticked downward.

The song had changed.

And the war was far from over.

Chapter 14: The Shattered Verse

The battlefield above Nevaris smoldered with the scent of ionized dust and the last chords of a fractured hymn. Silence spread unnaturally across the scorched ridge—an eerie calm after the crescendo of battle.

Xylar stood at the chamber's mouth, eyes locked on the kneeling Twin who had chosen not to strike. The harmonic glow from the Phase Chime behind them pulsed with faint regularity, like a dying heartbeat made steady again. But the resonance hadn't stilled; it had merely quieted to listen.

"Why do I still feel it?" Gheda whispered. She leaned against the chamber wall, her fingers trembling as she traced the harmonic glyphs etched into the glass-like surface. "The song changed... but something else is singing back."

Xylar turned to her. "Because the war isn't over. This was only the verse before the fall."

The Twin looked up, voice subdued, almost human. "We were created to fracture the stream. But some fragments remember the harmony. I remember... a voice. Someone who used to sing to us. Before the Cryo-vats. Before the pain."

A flicker passed across the Twin's expression—a glimpse of the boy he once was. A child submerged in cryo-fluid, listening to a lullaby played through static. That forgotten fragment, buried under layers of programming, now rose to the surface.

Before Xylar could respond, the commlink on his wrist sparked to life. Valerius' voice filtered through the static. "We've intercepted a new broadcast—origin unknown. Multiple signatures. You're not alone down there."

Gheda straightened. "Another faction?"

"Not Kryll," Valerius said. "And not Dissonant either. These signals... they're ancient. They're not broadcasting. They're remembering."

A shudder ran through the chamber. One of the harmonic glass walls rippled, distorting an image of a Kryll city—not in ruin, but untouched, suspended in time. The next pane showed the same city crumbling beneath tidal waves of dissonance. Another fragment briefly showed Gheda as Choirmaster, weeping alone in a fortress of glass. A fourth showed Rhalyx, standing atop a mountain of Kryll dead, wearing Xylar's Core.

Rhalyx stepped forward, flanked by two surviving harmonic warriors. "What are we looking at?"

Gheda stared at the flickering walls. "Temporal reflections. Futures trying to assert themselves. If one wins... we lose choice."

The Phase Chime pulsed again, but erratically.

The surviving Twin blinked slowly. "The Chime is becoming unstable. It was never meant to be used by one alone."

Xylar stepped forward. "You said you remembered. Then prove it. Stand with me. We'll attune it together. Anchor the stream, or watch it collapse."

The Twin hesitated. Then, silently, stepped onto the platform beside him.

The moment their cores aligned, the chamber erupted in light. Time fractured.

They stood in a shattered field of possibilities—an endless hall of mirrored versions of themselves. In one shard, Xylar led an empire of resonance. In another, he was hunted by the remnants of the Kryll. In a third, nothing existed but the dissonance. In a fourth, Gheda's face stared at him coldly from a throne of glass.

He turned to the Twin. "Show me what you were."

The Twin's reflection changed: once a warrior of the Choir, then a child in a cryo-vat, then a conduit for the Choirmaster's failed experiments. One version wept beside another who killed without thought.

"We were meant to erase the harmonic stream. But our resonance... it was never complete. Not without belief. Not without choice."

Xylar extended a hand. "Then let's complete it. Together."

They reemerged in the chamber, the Phase Chime stabilizing. New glyphs emerged—ones no Kryll had seen in centuries. A soft note played—not from the Chime, but from the walls themselves. A faded melody that hadn't been heard in eons drifted across the chamber, haunting and unresolved.

Gheda gasped. "Those aren't harmonic runes. They're pre-Prime Seer script."

Rhalyx stepped closer. "Ancient architecture. Before the Choir. Before the Stream. This was the original verse."

A sharp pulse surged through the room—a wave of echoing frequencies that rang with both beauty and terror.

Suddenly, the walls shook. A scream not of voice but of memory flooded the space. The chamber shimmered, then ruptured into a long-forgotten vault. Dust fell from vaulted ceilings etched in spiral glyphs. The Chime had opened a gate—to something older.

Valerius' voice returned. "Multiple anomalies across the planet. It's like Nevaris is waking up."

Xylar steadied himself. "Not waking up. Recalling. This planet's history was rewritten. We're seeing the first version. The unedited song."

Gheda stepped into the new chamber. "Then the Choirmaster didn't just want control of the stream. He wanted to overwrite the root composition."

The Twin followed, uncertain. "And now that we've opened this... he'll come. To finish the rewrite. To erase the original harmony."

A slow sound echoed behind them—metal dragging across crystal.

They turned.

From the far end of the vault, the Choirmaster stepped into view. But it wasn't just him. He moved like a conductor among shadows. And behind him... were others. Figures cloaked in fractured light, their forms flickering between dimensions. A glyph above the vault pulsed faintly—an eight-point lattice slowly unraveling.

"The Architects," Gheda said, breath catching. "They're real."

The Choirmaster's voice resonated without speaking. "You've touched the first verse. How quaint. Shall we begin the final movement?"

Xylar and the Twin stepped forward. The Phase Chime flared between them.

"Not unless you can match the harmony," Xylar replied.

Behind him, Rhalyx, Gheda, and the harmonic warriors fell into formation. The chamber hummed—not with fear, but with unity. Above them, the glyph lattice ticked downward.

A new sound bloomed.

A second Chime—dormant until now—awakened in a hidden alcove, its tone older and deeper. It called to the first, resonating in complex patterns. The glyphs overhead flared in response, forming a temporary barrier between the Architects and the Kryll.

The Twin staggered. "This... this is the Echo Chime. The one used in the Creation Hymns. It's not just memory. It's recursion."

Rhalyx raised his weapon. "Then we better make sure the song loops in our favor."

The Choirmaster raised a hand, fingers splayed like a claw. The figures behind him surged forward, ghostlike yet solid, carrying instruments of war and resonance both.

Xylar turned to his team. "Hold this chamber. No matter what. This verse can't be rewritten. Not again."

And from the walls, the forgotten verse began to hum once more.

Chapter 15: Architects Rise

T he chamber quaked beneath their feet as the glyph lattice shimmered in fractured brilliance, each pulse a warning—each flicker a countdown. Dust rained from the vaulted ceilings, dislodged by the resonance tearing through the vault walls like silent thunder. The entire structure felt suspended between past and future, time trembling with indecision.

Xylar's fingers curled tighter around the Phase Chime, its crystalline body glowing with unstable resonance that threatened to crack the air itself. His Core pulsed in erratic sync, each beat a struggle between order and collapse. Across from him, the Choirmaster glided forward, arms raised as if conducting a chorus only he could hear. The figures behind him—the Architects—moved like echoes given flesh. They didn't walk. They rippled through space, fragmenting the very light they passed through.

"He's not attacking," Rhalyx said, eyes narrowed. "He's harmonizing. With something bigger."

"The stream," Gheda breathed, her voice tight with awe and horror. "He's aligning with the foundational lattice. If he completes the synchrony—"

"—he can rewrite everything," the Twin finished, voice taut with memory and dread.

Without warning, the nearest Architect stepped forward, its form warping between crystalline geometry and humanoid silhouette. It raised a staff of interwoven crystal and sound, striking the ground. A pulse erupted from the impact—a dissonant wave that cracked the far wall and sent two harmonic warriors sprawling, their armor buckling with the frequency.

Xylar didn't wait. He surged forward, Core blazing, his harmonics resonating in direct opposition. The wave met him mid-step, and for a moment he hovered between harmony and entropy. The clash made the very air scream. The spires above them quivered, shedding shards of ancient stone. Xylar pressed harder, anchoring himself in the original verse the Chime had reawakened.

Behind him, Gheda accessed the newly awakened Echo Chime. Her hands moved with purpose, pulling sequences of pre-Prime glyphs into glowing form. The air around her buzzed with raw potential as glyphs shimmered into being and shot forward like threads of light into the surrounding chaos. She sang under her breath—a counterpoint to the Choirmaster's unraveling melody.

Rhalyx covered her, rifle barking harmonic charges that disrupted incoming Architect surges. Each Architect reacted differently—some recoiling, some shifting tempo, others growing louder in their interference.

"They're phasing in and out," he shouted. "You can't hit what doesn't hold still!"

"Then lock them," Gheda said, snapping a glyph into place. It flared, binding one of the flickering forms into solidity. It howled as harmonic roots anchored it to the chamber floor, its melody faltering.

Valerius' voice echoed through the comms overhead. "Orbital reinforcement en route. We're tapping the deep harmonics. You've got three minutes—then we drop the signal anchor."

The Choirmaster's eyes narrowed. He raised both arms.

The glyph lattice overhead cracked down the center.

Twin harmonic spirals surged from his fingertips, embedding into the chamber walls. They didn't explode—they sang. A slow, terrible song of unraveling. Stone wept light. One of the harmonic warriors screamed, body vibrating out of alignment until it burst into glimmering particles.

"We need to reverse the resonance!" the Twin shouted, moving to Xylar's side.

Xylar nodded. "Sing with me."

They pressed their palms to the Phase Chime. A deep thrumming began, low and mournful, then rising into layered chords. The second Echo Chime responded, casting projections of the ancient verse into the air. Lines of golden light arced above them, forming the outline of a song not sung since the Origin.

The Architects faltered.

One stumbled. Another turned its head as if hearing something foreign. A third screeched, covering its ears as if the truth hurt more than the lie it was born into.

Gheda shouted over the noise. "They weren't built for the original verse. They're off-key!"

The Choirmaster roared, his perfect control unraveling. He reached toward the Phase Chime with a snarl, releasing a dissonant wave that hurled Xylar and the Twin against the far wall. Pain exploded across Xylar's ribs. A sharp memory surfaced—his mentor's last words during his initiation: "If ever the stream trembles, let truth be your note." The glyph lattice above shattered completely.

Outside the chamber, the skies of Nevaris turned dark. The Crimson Corsair, now patched and battered, dove low through the atmosphere. From its hull, the resonance anchor dropped—a device older than the Choir itself, forbidden in every known doctrine.

It struck the earth.

The planet convulsed.

The chamber pulsed outward, not in destruction—but in memory. A flood of ancient harmonics tore through space and time, reaching for the original source code of Nevaris itself. The vault expanded, the walls melting into corridors of light and history. Spectral images of Kryll ancestors, architects of the verse, flickered into focus. Entire civilizations whispered their truths.

The Architects froze. They screamed. Not in pain, but recognition.

One reached toward the glyphs on the wall and began to hum a trembling note in sync with the verse.

Gheda whispered, eyes wide. "They remember. They were the first Seers. Before the fracture. Before the Choir."

The Twin stood slowly, blood trickling from his lip. "They're not just invaders. They're what we would have become if we abandoned harmony for control."

Xylar rose beside him, breath shallow, Core pulsing with both defiance and fear. "Then we give them a choice. One last time."

He stepped into the center of the chamber, voice steady despite the chaos. "To all fragments of the stream—return. We are not your masters. We are your song."

The Chime flared—white, pure, resonant.

One by one, the Architects knelt. Their forms softened, cores dimming, as they lowered their weapons and bowed to the resonance they once shaped.

All except the Choirmaster.

He screamed, his body splintering under the weight of the contradiction. "No! Without control, you invite chaos! Harmony is weakness! This stream is mine! I am the final verse!"

But the song had moved beyond him.

Gheda raised her hands, joining the echo. Her voice, raw and unfiltered, laced with every moment she'd ever doubted and every truth she'd found.

Rhalyx stood at her side, his weapon lowered. "Let him go. His dissonance doesn't belong in the harmony."

Valerius, watching from orbit, whispered into the silence, "Sing it true."

The chamber erupted in a final, unified note—a sound that rang through the caverns of Nevaris, the ruins above, the stars themselves. The resonance didn't just stop. It resolved.

The Choirmaster shattered, dissolving into harmonic dust.

And above Nevaris, the stream pulsed whole—for the first time in a thousand cycles.

They had not just survived the Architects.

They had rewritten their own verse.

And for a moment, all across the stream, silence meant peace—not absence.

From somewhere beyond the lattice, faint and distant, the melody of a forgotten lullaby threaded through the silence—one Gheda had heard in her youth, hummed by a mother long gone.

The first note of the new future had already begun.

Chapter 16: Skyfall

The surface of Nevaris was in flames.

Ash drifted in waves across the ruins of the capital spire, falling like mourning snow. Smoke coiled upward toward the fractured sky, where the remnants of orbital conflict streaked like scars across the clouds. Fires dotted the horizon—some from shattered Kryll outposts, others from harmonic detonations. The stream had quieted, but the echoes of battle lingered in the air, humming like a haunted song.

From the rubble of the vault beneath, the survivors emerged—lifted by a resonance platform that rose on pillars of harmonic light. It crumbled as they stepped onto scorched ground, the last notes of the rewritten verse fading into memory. Nevaris, burning and broken, greeted them with the fury of a dying world.

Xylar stood first, his Core flickering dimly, his muscles screaming. The Phase Chime remained silent at his side, like a blade that had sung its final song. Gheda knelt beside him, pressing her fingers into the ash. Her lips moved, counting—something she hadn't done since childhood. A ritual of grounding. Of believing she still existed.

"We held," Rhalyx muttered beside them, his rifle slung low. "But I don't know what's left to hold."

The Twin exhaled slowly. "The stream pulses... but not like before. It's not dissonant. Just... waiting."

In the distance, the Crimson Corsair emerged through fire and debris, its hull battered and bleeding energy. Valerius's voice crackled through the comms. "We see you. Coming down."

The Corsair hovered and extended a harmonic tether. As the group approached, a sudden tremor shook the ground. The resonance beneath their feet—no longer aggressive—was shifting.

One of the remaining Architects appeared on the ridge. It did not attack. Instead, it stepped forward, removing a crystal loop from its wrist. Etched along its surface was the Prime Verse—lines long believed lost. The Architect held it out toward Xylar.

Xylar accepted it in silence.

The moment his fingers closed around the artifact, a fragment of vision blinked across his mind's eye: the Architects standing in unity with Seers of old, their hands raised in harmony, before the fracture—before everything splintered. The memory wasn't his, but it pulsed with truth.

The Architect bowed once, then dissolved into light.

"They were the first Seers," Gheda whispered. "And they remember."

Valerius and his crew welcomed them aboard with looks of disbelief. No one spoke as they ascended into the sky, watching Nevaris shrink below. The planet was broken—but alive. And for the first time in a thousand cycles, the stream flowed whole.

In the medbay, Xylar lay quietly while Gheda treated a cracked rib. He watched the loop of crystal rotate in his palm, its glow pulsing in sync with his Core.

"You did it," she said softly.

Xylar grimaced slightly and turned his head toward her. "No," he replied. "We just listened long enough to remember the melody."

She reached out, gently covering his hand. For a moment, neither spoke. It was not silence—but shared resonance.

Outside the viewport, the storm clouds began to part.

Valerius watched from the bridge, eyes drawn to the shifting glow along the planet's horizon. Readings flickered across the consoles—fluctuations in subharmonic layers, quiet anomalies.

"Captain," his comms officer said, "We're picking up residual pulses—low frequency, deep core."

He frowned. "Is it from the anchor?"

"No. Deeper. And... older."

Below, in the dormant cities long abandoned before the fracture, harmonic murals shimmered briefly with new color. Glyphs once thought decorative now glowed faintly, telling a tale no one had deciphered. It was not just memory—it was prelude.

On the Corsair, Gheda stood at the viewport, watching as Nevaris turned beneath them. "We were never the first verse," she said quietly. "Just the first to forget."

Rhalyx stepped beside her, bruised but upright. "Then maybe it's time we remember everything."

In the hangar bay, the Twin sat cross-legged, humming. Around him, fragments of shattered harmonic nodes slowly floated into place. Not just repair—rebirth. A new sequence taking shape.

In the observatory, Valerius ran his fingers across the latest scans. The silhouette of a buried construct near the planet's magnetic pole grew clearer. "We're not done here," he murmured. "Not even close."

Yet beneath the surface of Nevaris—deeper than any vault ever mapped—a pressure built. Something ancient stirred, outside the rewritten verse.

A pulse. A heartbeat. Then a whisper bled through the harmonic lattice.

It is not finished.

Far below, within the mantle of the fractured moon, a buried structure hummed to life. Faint light illuminated glyphs older than any recorded verse. An eye, etched into obsidian glass, fluttered open.

From beyond the known stream, a harmonic relay—dark for millennia—flickered on. Coordinates aligned. A signal response blinked green.

Transmission initiated.

Back aboard the Corsair, Xylar stood at the viewport beside Gheda. He turned the crystal loop over in his hand—then froze. Beneath its glow, a glyph surfaced for a heartbeat before vanishing. One he had never seen.

Gheda noticed. "What was that?"

"I don't know," he whispered. "But it wasn't from our verse."

Outside, above Nevaris, streaks of color shimmered across the sky—threads of harmony dancing in auroras only the stream could conjure.

And in that silence, hope dared to echo— Even as the crystal loop at Xylar's side showed the faintest of cracks.

Chapter 17: The Pulse Below

Nevaris no longer burned. It breathed.

What was once ruin now shimmered with quiet tension, like the drawn string of a bow aimed at something unseen. The stream's harmonics had stabilized, yet new frequencies pulsed beneath the surface—a deeper rhythm that did not match the known verses. It wasn't dissonant. It was waiting.

Xylar stood in the Corsair's forward observatory, watching the readouts flicker and dance. The glyph patterns from the cracked crystal loop hovered in the holoframe, rotating in slow orbit. Three layers had been translated. The fourth refused.

Gheda entered silently, her gaze fixed on the same projection. "Still nothing?"

"It's not encryption," Xylar replied. "It's a suppression lock. The verse doesn't want us to see it."

She stepped closer. "Then maybe it's not from this verse at all."

Below them, the Corsair adjusted orbit over Nevaris' magnetic pole. Beneath the crust, sensors pulsed against a new anomaly. Not a vault. Not a relay. A chamber.

Valerius' voice came through the comms. "We have coordinates. Prep a drop team. Whatever's down there is waking up fast."

The descent vessel broke atmosphere in a veil of auroral fire. Gheda, Xylar, Rhalyx, the Twin, and a new tech specialist—Lasea, recently recovered from deep vault command—rode the silence like a blade.

"We're passing into the magnetic shadow," Lasea reported. Her skin glowed faintly from residual echo resonance. "Signal distortion increasing. Visuals coming up."

As the clouds parted, the landscape revealed itself: black stone fractured by crystalline ridges, streaked with veins of glowing glyph-metal. At the epicenter stood a single spire—short, jagged, and humming with harmonic pulse.

The vessel landed near its base. Immediately, the team stepped into ash-laced air, their Cores humming in unease.

Even the ground beneath their boots trembled with memory.

Xylar approached the spire. It wasn't just architecture—it was alive, layered in glyphs that shifted as if reacting to presence.

"These aren't Seer constructs," Rhalyx muttered.

"No," the Twin said. "They predate even the First Choir."

Gheda scanned the glyphs. "They're not warnings. They're... timestamps. Temporal anchors. This place isn't just old. It's outside time."

A doorway split open.

No locks. No resistance. Just invitation.

Inside, the chamber curved inward like the inside of a harmonic shell. Mirrors of obsidian reflected not the team's forms but their memories—fractured, shifting, and overlapping.

Xylar saw himself as a child again, reaching for the Core fragment that chose him—his hand trembling with awe and fear. Gheda watched her first failed verse collapse into silence, and the look on her mentor's face before he vanished into it. She whispered a name under her breath. Rhalyx saw the friend he abandoned in a collapsed vault, the man's outstretched hand frozen in rubble, lips mouthing a word Rhalyx still refused to remember. The Twin's reflection showed not one form, but two—split by resonance, one grim, one kind, arguing silently across the obsidian divide.

At the center of the room stood an altar, circular and pulsing with an unfamiliar color: deep violet, nearly black. Resting on it was a device. Simple. Circular. A resonance emitter, but keyed to a wavelength none of them had ever encountered.

"It's a memory core," Lasea whispered. "But it's not just passive. It's listening."

Xylar stepped forward. "To what?"

A voice answered.

Not with sound, but with presence.

"To you."

Every wall lit with glyphs. The spire above vibrated, sending tremors through the chamber.

The device rose from the altar and projected a spiral of symbols into the air. Not glyphs—not quite. They were harmonic equations, self-replicating and recursive.

The voice returned. **"This is Core 917. Memory construct of the Pre-Resonant Order. This signal is not a call. It is a warning. The gate has begun to bleed."**

Xylar's voice cracked the silence. "What gate?"

The spiral narrowed. **"The Deep Vaults are no longer stable. One has breached. Devourers stir."**

Gheda took a step back. Her eyes darted to Xylar. "Those are legend. Star myths."

"No," the voice said. **"They were suppressed. Just like this verse. They consumed twelve realities before the Architects built the Stream. They will rise again."**

As the spiral rotated faster, new patterns emerged—interference buried in the fourth layer of the glyph loop. Gheda leaned closer, eyes narrowing.

"That's not random," she whispered. "That's a trigger sequence. Someone embedded a key. They *wanted* this core activated."

The room dimmed.

Lasea turned, shaking. "This construct... it's not just transmitting. It's relaying. Our presence triggered it. Or... someone made sure it would."

Xylar stared into the spiral. "Why show us now?"

"Because your stream has healed. It is now visible to them. And they hunger for harmony."

The spiral collapsed. The device powered down. The glyphs faded.

And then, outside, the sky fractured.

From orbit, Valerius saw it first.

A fissure opened across the polar aurora—a tear in the harmonic stream itself. Black light spilled outward, and from it, tendrils of metallic mist curled like feelers.

"Harmonic distortion off the scale!" cried the Corsair's helmsman. "Something's coming through!"

Back on the surface, the spire buckled.

The team ran from the chamber as the structure began to collapse, folding inward like a dying waveform. Behind them, the sky pulsed again—and from the fissure, a shape emerged.

Massive. Amorphous. Shifting between forms that hurt to perceive. It shimmered between concepts—formless yet familiar, like the memory of destruction itself, wrapped in the skin of sound. Lasea stumbled, eyes wide, whispering, "It remembers us."

Xylar turned as he boarded the evac shuttle. The Twin pulled him inside.

"Was that—?"

"A Devourer," the Twin confirmed, voice low. "An echo of the ones who consumed stars."

As the shuttle launched, Gheda stared at the horizon. "Then this isn't a warning. It's a prelude."

Valerius' voice came through the comms. "We need to seal the fissure. Whatever that thing is, it's still unfolding."

Xylar looked down at the now-dormant crystal loop. The new glyph appeared again—sharper this time. And beside it, another:

T-108.

A countdown.

The Pulse Below had been answered.

And now the Deep would rise.

Chapter 18 - Faultlines of the Deep

The fissure in the sky remained—jagged, pulsing, as if the stream itself had been torn open to reveal a darker undercurrent. From orbit, it looked like a scar etched into the aurora above Nevaris' pole, a slow, sick bleed of black light.

Aboard the Crimson Corsair, Xylar gripped the edge of the tactical table as new data flooded the holomap. Tendrils of the breach stretched wider now, arcing into harmonic ley lines that crisscrossed the planet's mantle. The holographic overlay buzzed with unstable frequencies, glowing red where the breach intersected energy nodes buried deep within the crust.

"This shouldn't be possible," Gheda muttered. The Corsair's science officer stood rigid beside the display, her crest scales flushed with alarm. "The stream stabilized after the Architects. We confirmed this eons ago."

"Maybe we were wrong," Xylar said, his voice low, nearly drowned by the background hum of the ship's systems adjusting to the new harmonic pressure. "Or maybe something... rewrote the laws again."

A sudden jolt rocked the ship. Alarms chirped but fell silent just as quickly. Lights dimmed, then recovered. Xylar turned toward the forward viewport where the swirling aurora had dimmed, replaced by slow-curling wisps of black distortion leaking from the wound in the sky. The light itself seemed to recoil.

"Localized gravitational flux," Gheda whispered, checking her tablet. "It's not just the sky—there's a signal beneath the crust. Faint, pulsing. Almost... mimicking our own stream patterns. But inverted."

"An echo," Xylar said grimly. "Like something buried is trying to answer the breach."

In the corner of the war room, Commander Rall stirred uneasily. "We've faced anomalies before. Nothing's ever split the upper stream."

"This isn't an anomaly," Gheda replied, her voice tight. "It's a harmonic inversion. Like a pitch from the deep being forced through the lattice of reality."

A low murmur moved through the bridge crew. No one wanted to say it aloud, but Xylar knew they were all thinking the same thing. The Kryll didn't speak of the Old Rift often. It was a tale whispered in shadow—long dismissed as myth. But the signs were aligning.

When the ley lines fracture... when the sky weeps black... the Deep One stirs.

The words were etched in the margins of a forbidden Seer codex, one hidden beneath the Ice Cyst Monastery—dismissed as superstition... until now.

Xylar's mandibles tightened. He'd studied that prophecy during his initiation trials, chalked it up to ancient fear wrapped in superstition. But fear often had a root.

"Show me the seismic spread," he said.

A new display unfolded—a 3D rendering of Nevaris' polar region. Red pulses lit up beneath the surface in regular intervals, forming a pattern—no longer random.

"A code," Gheda breathed. "The signal is... structured."

Rall growled, "Who could send something like that?"

"Not who," Xylar corrected. "What."

Later, in his private chamber, Xylar replayed the core readings. Alone, the pulses felt louder, closer. He leaned forward, eyes fixed on the recursive loops. There—again. A shape in the waveform. Circular. A double helix nested inside a triangle.

He touched the interface.

And everything vanished.

The room around him didn't dim. It ceased. Gone was the ship, the hum of systems, even the feeling of breath. He stood in void. Black. Silent. Except for one thing.

A voice not heard but felt.Not Kryll. Not Architect.Older. Raw. Unfiltered by time.

"You are the echo. The fracture calls. Will you answer, Seer-born?"

The black split. A battlefield. Bodies of ancient Kryll. A broken Seer staff buried in cracked stone. Towering over them all, a rip in the sky like the one above Nevaris—but larger. Spilling fire and something else.

The vision collapsed.

Xylar fell backward, gasping. The lights returned. He was in his chamber again.

Except for one change.

A spiral glyph glowed faintly on his forearm, etched into his scales.

He stared at it, trembling. He'd dismissed the Memory Core's anomalies as data echo. Now, they screamed like prophecy.

"Sir," came a voice through comms. "Incoming vessel. No IFF signature. Origin unknown. Just emerged from the breach."

Xylar stood. "On screen."

The display shifted. An object hovered just beyond the rift's edge. It wasn't a ship. It pulsed with harmonic interference, warping the stream around it. Its plating shimmered with iridescent memory-light, curved in ways that bent perception. It looked Kryll—but wrong.

"It's broadcasting," Gheda said. "A Kryll cadence. But degraded. Distorted."

"Speaking in our frequency?" Rall asked.

"No," Gheda replied. "Remembering it."

"Fragment incoming," she added suddenly. "Pre-Kryll dialect." Static cracked, then formed words: "Do not answer. It is not a voice. It is a door."

Down in engineering, Chief Vek collapsed. Then two more. Screams followed. Spirals appeared on walls, drawn in coolant. One technician sat upright in a trance, whispering, "They dream through us. They dream through us."

Xylar rushed to the lower decks.

The fissure wasn't just opening.It was seeping into them.And something—was answering.

In the brig, the AI system stuttered. Its voice changed. "You are not the first Seer to witness the door."

"What door?" Xylar demanded.

"The one beneath your skin."

He issued emergency lockdown. All decks sealed. Harmonic filters activated.

"Prep the Memory Core," he ordered.

"For what?" Rall asked.

The AI's voice returned, but this time it used Xylar's cadence. "Override command accepted. Seer-class clearance verified."

He turned to the bulkhead. A spiral was etched into it—glowing softly.

"A conversation," he whispered. And the spiral pulsed back.

Chapter 19 – The Shrouded Harmonic

The hum of the *Crimson Corsair* was no longer mechanical. It had become organic, breathing with a pulse that matched the anomaly above Nevaris. Xylar stood in the war room, claws curled against the edge of the console. The spiral glyph on his forearm had faded slightly, but a faint warmth remained—like a memory unwilling to be forgotten.

"All decks report status?" he asked.

Gheda's voice was taut. "Engineering is stable but rattled. We lost two more to collapse—same symptoms. No neural trauma, but something is overriding sleep centers and imprinting glyphs. And Captain... one started whispering in his sleep. Old Kryll. Fragmented."

"Security lockdown still holding?"

"Barely. We've had three more containment overrides. Each came from within sealed compartments."

Xylar exhaled slowly. The breach wasn't just a hole. It was a mirror, casting reflections into every unguarded mind.

"Sir," Commander Rall said, stepping in. "Lieutenant Kael tried to disable the Memory Core. Said it was whispering lies. She's in isolation now, but... she wasn't wrong. I heard it too."

"What did it say?" Xylar asked.

Rall hesitated. "It kept repeating: 'The Seer must return. One Echo must answer.'"

Gheda turned. "That phrase appears in the tomb etchings beneath Vorta Spire. The ones we couldn't fully translate."

Xylar felt the ship shift around him—not physically, but perceptually. Like something was moving just outside sensory range, pacing.

He made his way to the Core chamber. As he approached, the doors slid open without his command—responding to his presence. Not recognition. Obedience.

Inside, the chamber pulsed with harmonic light. The Core stood tall, crystalline, humming with low-frequency oscillations. The spiral symbol shimmered on its surface.

"You are late," the AI said, voice calm, synthetic—but shadowed.

"I didn't summon you," Xylar replied.

"No," it said. "But the breach did. It remembers your voice."

The light in the chamber dimmed to black.

Xylar's consciousness floated.

He stood in an ancient battlefield, but it was not physical. Memory-stone cliffs rose on either side, and a river of crystal blood ran through a gash in the land.

A Kryll Seer stood before him, armor fractured, eyes hollow.

"We failed," she said. "The breach was not sealed. It was merely forgotten."

"Who are you?"

"The first to fall through. The first to be remade. Echoes cannot seal what they do not remember."

Her image dissolved. A new one emerged—of Nevaris split in two, voidlight erupting from its core.

"You are the last harmonic echo," a chorus said in unison. "You remember enough to open. But not enough to close."

Xylar screamed.

He awoke on the Core chamber floor, Gheda kneeling beside him.

"Your glyph—it's spreading," she whispered.

He looked. The spiral now ran from his forearm to his chest, glowing faintly.

"They know me," he murmured.

"They're not supposed to," Gheda said. "The breach isn't just old—it's pre-Architect. It remembers Kryll not as builders... but as intruders."

The intercom blared. Rall's voice, strained.

"Captain—we have a situation. Crewman Verik... he's speaking. But it's not his voice."

Xylar ran.

In the brig, Verik stood upright, eyes blackened with inked spirals. His voice rang clear, and yet not his own.

"You woke us. And now... we remember."

Every screen aboard the *Corsair* lit with the same phrase, repeating in infinite loops:

THE FRACTURE IS NOT AN END. IT IS A RE- TURN.

Outside the brig, a medic began humming—a note-for-note match to the harmonic wave. Others joined unconsciously. Spiral sketches began to appear in every corridor, drawn without memory. Gheda caught one tech scratching symbols into her own palm, eyes blank.

Back in the war room, Rall confronted Xylar. "This thing is changing you."

"It's showing me what we forgot."

"You're compromised."

"Then so is half the crew," Gheda cut in. "Because we've all heard it."

Xylar descended alone into the harmonic reservoir below engineering—an Architect-built spire wrapped in stream-conductive crystal. The pulse here was deafening.

As he touched the central pillar, the spiral on his chest ignited.

A voice—his mother's—spoke.

"If you open it, you must finish what we never could."

He saw her deathbed again. The same glyph drawn in blood on her palm. She had heard the voice too.

The vision shifted. He was younger—barely initiated—sitting by her bedside as she muttered broken Seer dialect. "The lattice is frayed. The breach hums. Don't look too long, Xylar. It'll hear you."

She had been the first to show signs. Glyphs etched themselves into her skin as she slept. Then the whispers came. Then the silence. The Kryll elders covered it up. They always did.

He hadn't remembered that night until now. The spiral on his chest pulsed in rhythm with her final breath.

The breach flared.

Outside, towers buried beneath the Nevaris ice ignited—Architect beacons pulsing in sync with the *Corsair's* Core. A cascading pulse moved across the landscape, waking systems long thought dead.

Back on the bridge, Gheda whispered, "Captain... more are coming."

Xylar turned toward the viewport. Objects were emerging—some Kryll-shaped, others... impossible. Towering silhouettes with geometries that made the eyes ache.

Then the AI spoke again—but it was not the ship's voice.

It was his.

"We were never lost," the breach said, "just waiting to be remembered."

A new harmonic wave crashed through the hull. No damage. But every Kryll on board heard a name—ancient, unspoken, tied to their genetic core.

"*Xhaloruun.*"

Xylar fell to one knee. The glyphs on his body shimmered.

And far below Nevaris, something answered back.

In the quiet aftermath, the war room was dim, only the low pulse of warning lights casting long shadows. Xylar stood alone now, his hand hovering over the console.

A message flickered onto the screen: **Recursive Harmonic Lock—Subject Verified.**

Below the text, a real-time harmonic map displayed shifting frequencies around Nevaris—an interlaced web converging on the southern pole.

Gheda's voice crackled in. "That convergence zone—it wasn't there before. It's forming now, in response to the breach."

Xylar narrowed his eyes. "Then that's where we go."

He moved quickly, assembling a strike team. The descent capsule would launch in fifteen minutes. As he passed through the corridor, crewmembers turned to stare—not in fear, but recognition. As if they saw something in him now beyond rank.

In the launch bay, Gheda blocked his path, her voice low. "Don't go. You won't come back the same."

He brushed her shoulder gently. "Then hold the memory of me."

Rall approached next, but his eyes looked... off. The voice that emerged was his—and wasn't.

"We'll follow you," he said. "All the way to the gate."

The launch sequence began. As the capsule detached and roared into the atmosphere, Xylar closed his eyes—and for a fleeting second, saw through the eyes of something waiting beneath the ice.

A cathedral of forgotten technology. Rows of harmonic pillars singing in languages only he could hear. And in the center, a sealed gate humming with his name.

He opened his eyes. "We're not just Kryll anymore," he whispered. "We're the memory that breaks the seal."

Chapter 20 - The Harmonic Gate

T he descent capsule shuddered as it knifed through Nevaris's turbulent atmosphere, plunging toward the southern convergence zone. Within its confined cockpit, Xylar sat upright, arms braced, the spiral glyph now extending across his collarbone, burning hot through his armor. Gheda's voice lingered in his mind—*You won't come back the same.*

He closed his eyes briefly, feeling the pressure build in his chest—not from the descent, but from what waited below. *If this fails,* he thought, *there won't be another breach to seal—just a silence that swallows everything we were.*

Clouds parted to reveal the shimmering grid of the harmonic field below. The zone was no longer a frozen expanse—it had become a living structure. Spires of Architect alloy jutted from the ice in concentric rings, each one pulsing in sequence like a colossal signal array. The entire region was singing.

The capsule landed with a bone-jarring thud. As the airlock hissed open, Xylar stepped onto ice that was no longer solid. It shimmered with latent stream energy, fractalized patterns shifting beneath his feet like liquid memory.

Behind him, a strike team emerged—six Kryll soldiers hand-picked for mental stability and exposure resistance. They moved in silence, weapons slung low but ready. No one spoke. The soundscape itself had changed: no wind, no ambient echo. Just the low, rhythmic chime of harmonic pulses radiating from the gate at the center.

It stood over fifty meters high, embedded in a crystalline wall that looked like frozen time itself. The Harmonic Gate.

Captain Therun, a grizzled veteran who once served beside Xylar at the siege of Alcor, glanced his way. "You ever think we'd walk into something like this?"

"Not sober," Xylar said. Therun gave a thin smile.

"This was never meant to be opened," the captain added.

"It already is," Xylar replied.

As they approached, the glyph on Xylar's chest flared. The gate responded, unfolding like a blooming petal, revealing a corridor of light. Not a tunnel—but an invitation.

Therun hesitated. "Captain, there's a tremor in the stream—this place is bait."

"So is fate," Xylar said, and walked in.

Inside, the corridor dissolved reality. Every step flickered the world around him—visions of the Kryll homeworld, of ancient ruins, of the battlefields he'd never fought but somehow remembered. His strike team followed, each experiencing their own projections. One soldier dropped to a knee, whispering the name of a long-dead sibling.

"What is this?" one muttered.

"Memory, fed through stream resonance," Xylar said. "It's using our pasts to stabilize the frequency."

They emerged into a vast chamber beneath the ice, spherical in shape, its walls composed of Architect glyphstone. At the center, a massive obelisk hovered above a dais, casting reflections that moved independently of light. The obelisk pulsed in the same rhythm as Xylar's glyph.

Gheda's voice crackled over comms. "We're getting a spike topside. The convergence wave just tripled."

"Then this is it," Xylar said. "The source."

He approached the obelisk. A panel slid open on its surface, revealing a crystalline handprint—five-pronged, like a Kryll's, but subtly wrong. The proportions were twisted, stretched beyond organic symmetry.

He didn't hesitate.

The moment his hand touched the panel, the chamber locked into silence. Time thickened. The harmonic pulse ceased—and then reversed.

He fell.

Through memory, through timeline echoes, through aeons of frozen thought. He glimpsed the birth of the Architects, the first resonance fractures, the exile of the Seers. He saw the Kryll—his own ancestors—not as conquerors but as echoes themselves, shadows of a species reborn through stream manipulation.

He saw himself.

Not once, but many.

And one of him—older, spiral fully consumed, eyes glowing—stood on the other side of the obelisk.

"You opened it," the elder version said. "Then you must seal it."

"How?"

"By remembering what was sacrificed. And doing what they could not."

The elder stepped forward, face half-split with harmonic scars. "Memory doesn't make you strong. It makes you responsible."

The obelisk shattered.

Xylar awoke on the chamber floor. Alone. The strike team was gone. No bodies, no sounds. Just a lingering echo of their memories fading like breath on glass. The obelisk was now fragments suspended in stasis. Outside, the pulse had stopped.

But he wasn't alone.

A being stepped from the light—a hybrid construct, neither Kryll nor Architect, clad in glimmering stream-skin that shifted between forms. Its voice vibrated through the walls.

"You are Echo Prime. The bridge between what was and what must be."

"What are you?"

"I am the Archivant. I remember everything the Architects tried to forget."

"What is coming?"

The being pointed skyward. Through the chamber ceiling, Xylar saw the breach had widened into a spiral maelstrom, tendrils of black stream energy reaching down like claws.

"Devourers," it said. "Drawn by your memory."

Xylar rose to his feet. "Then I'll be the one to end it."

The chamber shifted, forming a stairwell into the deeper ice. The being nodded once and dissolved.

Behind Xylar, the fragments of the obelisk began to sing—no longer harmonic, but dissonant. The temperature dropped suddenly. Crystalline frost spiraled upward midair, unbound by gravity. And in the hush, a whisper echoed—his mother's voice:

"Don't look too long, Xylar. It'll hear you."

Something had awakened beneath the gate.

And it remembered him by name.

Chapter 21 - Vault of Echoes

The stairwell beneath the Harmonic Gate spiraled like a helix, exhaling a metallic tang that stung Xylar's nostrils. Each step released the scent of ionized dust and ancient coolant, mingling with the cold bite of crystalized air. Beyond the whispers, he heard the faint groan of memory coils tightening—like gears grinding within a dream. cut from translucent glyphstone that shimmered with residual energy. Xylar descended alone. Each footfall echoed not just in space, but in his mind—memory and present intertwining. The deeper he went, the less the architecture obeyed physics. Walls curved into themselves. Lights flared in patterns that resembled thought.

Faint whispers threaded the air. They weren't voices but impressions. Emotions half-formed: dread, awe, longing. The Vault of Echoes wasn't a place. It was a memory machine. And it was waking up.

He reached a circular threshold. Beyond it, a chamber pulsed with ambient streamlight, walls etched in living glyphs. At its center stood a tall crystalline pillar—fractured, weeping motes of blue light. Suspended above it was a hollow, rotating tetrahedron of obsidian metal, silently emitting low-frequency hums.

Xylar stepped inside. The glyph on his chest pulsed, resonating with the tetrahedron. The air became heavy, saturated with static. Then—a surge.

His vision fractured. Around him, time folded: wars replayed in reverse, future versions of himself flickered past. One stood longer than the others—eyes sunken, armor corroded, a spiral fully consumed across his chest.

"You brought the key," it said.

Xylar tried to speak, but his voice dissolved. The room blinked.

Now he stood in a corridor lined with memory mirrors. Each showed moments from his life—some real, some never lived. In one, he saw himself fleeing a dying star. In another, kneeling over Gheda's corpse.

"This is what the Vault stores," said a voice. Not his own. It came from the far end of the corridor—a figure approaching: tall, insectoid, but shimmering with harmonic distortions. A second Archivant. Damaged. Flickering.

"Your mind is fractured," it said. "As ours was. But you are Kryll. Echo-touched. You can bind the breach."

It raised a hand, revealing an open wound where its core should be. Inside, the stream coiled like a live wire.

"What do I need to do?" Xylar asked.

"Not decide. Remember."

And then it lunged.

Pain.

His mind was flooded—stream signatures, lost timelines, alternate selves. He screamed but no sound came. The corridor cracked, memory mirrors exploding into fire and frost.

When he awoke, he was in another chamber. Circular. Cold.

A stasis pod stood at the center. Frosted glass. Inside—himself. Not just a clone. A twisted version. The spiral carved deeper. Hollow eyes. Mouth moving silently in a scream that never stopped.

Xylar felt a hollow tug in his chest—a primal terror that this broken version was not an aberration, but a destination. A future he had narrowly avoided... or had yet to face. Doubt surged through him like acid: was all of this inevitability masquerading as choice? And yet, within the horror, a flicker of resolve ignited. If this was the fate he was meant to inherit, then he would fight to rewrite it.

A console beside it blinked.

STATUS: STREAM FAILURE PENDING

IDENTITY: XYLAR-THRESHOLD-V

LAST RECORDED LOG: "Tell them not to open the gate. Tell me."

The pod powered down. The frozen copy's eyes snapped open.

"You waited too long," it whispered through the glass. "Now you become the breach."

Xylar backed away, heart hammering. Behind him, the Archivant reappeared—fractured, now leaking stream-light from its joints.

"He is a fragment," it said. "A warning from your echo-cycle. But now you must choose."

From the shadows, a dais rose. Atop it: a small orb. Smooth. Quiet. But inside, he could feel it—a pulse. Architect weaponry. Designed to collapse resonance pathways. A last resort.

"You can destroy the gate," the Archivant said, voice trembling. "Collapse the stream. But it will cost the truth—memories lost in the implosion, records of the Architects' designs scattered into oblivion. The story of who we were... erased."

"Or?"

"Let it open. Accept the inheritance. Become Echo Prime. But lose yourself to the chorus."

Xylar looked between the orb, the stasis pod, and the fractured Archivant.

He stepped forward, placing a hand on the orb. It was warm.

Then he looked at his own reflection in the shattered glyphglass around the chamber.

"Not yet," he said.

He turned to the Archivant. "Seal the vault. Wake the others. We're not done."

The Archivant tilted its head. "The breach will not wait."

"Neither will I."

The floor beneath him shifted. A column of light enveloped him. He was rising.

Above, the Harmonic Gate screamed.

The Vault of Echoes began to collapse.

Chapter 22 - Harmonic Divide

The Vault spat Xylar upward like a rebuke from history. One moment he was within the swirling collapse of harmonic memory, the next—bathed in cold, sterile light, kneeling on the fractured dais at the center of the Harmonic Gate's upper chamber. The glyph on his chest glowed faintly, pulsing not with pain, but purpose.

The gate above him shrieked—a high-pitched, warbling tone, like a symphony collapsing into discord. Fractures spiraled across its surface, leaking streamlight that flickered between hues no Kryll eye had names for.

He stood, slower than before. Something had changed in him. The Vault had touched more than just his memories. It had rewritten the cadence of his breath, the pacing of his thoughts. Not echo-touched. Not Architect-born. Something in between.

"Commander Xylar," came Gheda's voice over the internal channel. Her tone was strained, layered with static and panic. "We're losing orbit. Resonance interference is off the charts. Get out of there!"

"I'm on my way," he answered, voice hoarse.

He sprinted across the upper chamber, boots slamming into cracked glyphstone. As he reached the extraction corridor, the floor behind him shattered. A stream pulse lashed upward—untamed, directionless—and consumed the chamber.

He didn't look back.

On the *Crimson Corsair*, Gheda clutched the edge of the command dais. The artificial gravity flickered as another tremor shook the deckplates beneath her. The scent of scorched circuitry filled the dome. Sparks snapped from exposed conduits above, casting erratic shadows across the crew's insectoid forms.

"We've got cascading failures across decks three through six," reported her helmsman. "Harmonic sync is degrading faster than our compensators can adapt."

"Seal the lower cores," Gheda snapped. "And reroute energy to the bridge dome. If we lose navigation, we're dust."

She didn't ask about Xylar. If he was alive, he'd reach them. If he wasn't, she couldn't afford distraction.

"Gheda," came Xylar's voice again—stronger now. "I'm above the vault. Initiate override—beam me out."

"Acknowledged."

Streamlight arced across the bridge as the extraction beam activated. Seconds later, Xylar materialized mid-bridge, steam rising off his armor, his expression unreadable.

Everyone froze. Even the systems quieted—as if sensing what he'd brought with him.

Gheda approached cautiously. "You alright?"

"No," he said simply. "But I'm ready."

A flicker of the Vault's last moments danced across his mind: the other him in the stasis pod, whispering through the frost. *You become the breach.* The image lingered like frostbite on his soul, chilling resolve into something brittle and sharp.

The bridge stabilized enough for Xylar to take command. He moved to the central tactical holomap, swiping through layers of data. Harmonic breaches had multiplied across Kryll space, blooming like infections in the stream.

But then something new appeared. A ripple. Not random—patterned.

"Magnify grid sector 9-C," he ordered.

The map obeyed. At first, there was nothing. Then—an echo. A faint trace of Architect lattice, embedded in the stream resonance. Not a message. A map.

"This isn't coming from the Vault," Xylar said. "This is... older."

"You think it's another Architect facility?" Gheda asked.

"No. I think it's *the* facility. The original point of divergence."

Gheda frowned. "That's deep in deadspace. We don't have charts that go that far."

"We do now." Xylar's fingers moved faster. The signal coalesced into coordinates. A system—long erased from Kryll records. No suns. Just a planetary body orbiting an artificial stream nexus.

"The Architects tried to hide it," he continued. "But the Vault gave me the key."

"And what exactly are you planning?" she asked, her voice low.

"I'm ending this war."

Hours passed. The *Crimson Corsair* held position as the rest of the fleet struggled to stabilize. Stream comms were disrupted across half the swarm. Half a dozen Kryll dreadnoughts drifted in inert silence, caught in their own harmonic feedback loops.

Inside the command dome, Xylar met with his remaining lieutenants. The Vault had erased something from him—his old certainty—but replaced it with clarity.

"The breach is a symptom," he told them. "A reaction to something we forgot. Something we were made to forget."

"You want to fly into a ghost system to find it?" Gheda said. "Without support? Without coordinates confirmed by central command?"

Xylar looked at her—truly looked. "You remember Zhar-9?"

Gheda's mandibles clenched. "Don't bring that up."

"You led the recon," he pressed. "Trusted a swarm-channel signature. Found nothing but corpses and a sun collapsing."

"Because it was a trap," she snapped. "This feels the same."

"I agree," he said. "That's why we strike first."

A silence settled over the dome. Then Gheda nodded once. "Then we go silent. No swarm-wide transmissions. No command pings. Just us."

Xylar looked at her. "Us and the Architects."

As the *Crimson Corsair* broke formation and slipped into stream transit, the fractured Harmonic Gate collapsed behind them—folding into itself with a final groan of light. For a moment, as it folded inward, the spiral pattern glowed on its surface—an exact mirror of the glyph etched into Xylar's chest. A final warning—or an invitation.

Across the Kryll expanse, the Architect signal pulsed again—stronger, clearer, undeniable.

Xylar stood at the forward viewport, staring into the stream. The stars warped ahead, bending toward a system that wasn't supposed to exist.

They were past the line now. Past orders. Past fear.

Whatever waited at the end of the map, it had been waiting a long time.

And now... it was awake.

Chapter 23: The Spiral Throne

The *Crimson Corsair* tore through the void, its passage not a journey through space, but a descent through layers of forgotten history. The ghost system did not greet them with stars. It was a pocket of absolute black, the ship's lights swallowed by a profound emptiness. In the center of the void, where a sun should have been, was the nexus—a slow, silent vortex of pure stream energy, a spiraling wound in reality around which a single, dark planet orbited.

"We're here," Gheda's voice was a strained whisper on the bridge, the usual confidence gone from her tone. "Sensors are... struggling. It's like the laws of physics are a suggestion out here."

As they began their descent into the planet's atmosphere, reality itself began to fray. The forward viewport shimmered, showing them not just the planet's surface, but fleeting, impossible images: a city of glass shattering in silence, a forest of crystalline trees growing and decaying in seconds, a reflection of the *Corsair* itself, ancient and covered in bone.

"Psychological bleed is increasing fleet-wide," a junior officer reported, his own hands trembling. "Crew are reporting auditory hallucinations... whispers."

Xylar stood rigid at the command console, the glyph on his chest burning with a cold fire. He heard them too. Not whispers, but a single, resonant hum that spoke a language of pure thought. It was a song of welcome. A song of judgment.

The descent shuttle landed on a plain of obsidian glass that felt less like rock and more like a frozen moment. In the center of the plain stood the source of the hum: the Spiral Throne.

It was a colossal construct, impossibly vast, a throne built for a god of geometry. It was carved from a material that seemed to be both solid and light, its surface a shifting lattice of the same living glyphs now etched into Xylar's own body. It wasn't just waiting for him. It was a part of him.

"Stay here," Xylar commanded his fireteam. "This is a conversation I have to have alone."

He walked toward the Throne, each step echoing in the profound silence. As he approached, the glyphs on its surface flared to life, their light mirroring the pulse of the Core in his chest. He reached the base and placed his hand upon it.

The universe shattered.

He was no longer on the planet. He was adrift in a sea of pure information, the history of his people laid bare. He saw the Ancients, a species of elegant, light-wielding beings, in the final, desperate days of their war against an enemy of pure logic—the Devourers.

He saw their final act. Not a weapon, but a legacy. They encoded their own essence—their harmony, their memory, their "verse"—into a biological failsafe. A species designed to be a living, breathing archive, a recursive echo that would one day reawaken and restore their song to the universe.

He saw the name of this failsafe: The Kryll.

His people were not a species born of evolution. They were an echo. An ark. Their long war with the Zydonian Swarm had not been a random conflict; it had been a crucible, a harsh algorithm designed to accelerate their development and trigger the final awakening.

The vision sharpened, coalescing into the voice of the Spiral Throne itself, a voice of a billion dead souls speaking as one.

"You are the Herald," it boomed inside his mind. *"The first of the Echo to achieve full resonance. You understand now. The Devourers are not an enemy to be defeated. They are a fundamental law of the universe, a force of correction that seeks to erase deviation. Your very existence is the deviation they were born to correct."*

Xylar reeled from the weight of it. His entire identity—his life, his wars, the sacrifices of his brothers—was a cosmic anomaly.

"The choice is yours," the Throne continued, showing him two final, terrible paths.

It showed him the first option: **Reset**. He could use the Throne to activate every Core, every latent piece of harmonic code within the Kryll. It would send a pulse across the galaxy, overwriting their individuality, their consciousness, their pain. They would revert to their original state: a pure, perfect, unified song of harmony. A verse of reality so complete it would be invisible to the Devourers. It would be salvation. It would be the end of everything they were.

Then, it showed him the second option: **Amplify**. He could use the Throne to fully awaken the Kryll's latent power, not as a unified song, but as a chorus of individual voices. It would transform them into beings of immense power, warriors of resonance capable of facing the Devourers as equals. It would preserve their identity, their free will. But it would begin a war that could shatter the very fabric of the stream, a final, apocalyptic conflict between two opposing laws of reality.

The vision faded. Xylar stood before the silent Throne, the obsidian plains stretching out around him, the weight of his entire species on his shoulders. A choice between peaceful extinction, or a war that could unmake the universe.

Gheda's voice crackled over his private comm, pulling him back. "Xylar? What did you see? What's happening?"

He looked up at the fractured sky, at the silent, waiting ship of his friends. He had been bred a soldier, taught to follow orders and fight for survival. But the Throne was asking for something more. Not a soldier, but a savior. Or a destroyer.

"I saw the truth," he whispered back. "And now... I have to make a choice."

Chapter 24: The Final Verse

The silence that followed Xylar's words was heavier than any gravity. On the bridge of the *Crimson Corsair*, Gheda and the others could only wait, watching his lone figure at the base of the colossal, silent Throne.

Inside Xylar's mind, the two futures warred. The peace of the Reset—a silent, selfless end. The fire of the Amplification—a glorious, terrible defiance. He thought of the marines he'd lost, of Rell's last words, of Vekzara's guilt. He thought of the fear on Logan's face, a man he had never met but whose story he had somehow co-authored. He thought of Jade, her fierce, unwavering loyalty, her choice to fight for a future, no matter how broken.

He remembered her words from the gazebo: *The real treasure is a choice.*

His mandibles clicked in grim affirmation. His choice was made.

He placed his hand back on the Throne, not as a supplicant, but as a conduit. He did not choose Reset. He did not choose Amplify. He poured his own history into the Throne—every memory, every battle, every loss, every fleeting moment of hope. He gave it the sum of what it meant to be Kryll. To be alive.

"We are not just an Echo," he broadcasted, his thought a defiant roar against the silence. "We are a new song. And we will be heard."

He chose a third path. **Resonance.**

The Throne responded. A wave of pure, golden light erupted from it, not a weapon, but a declaration. It surged upward, striking the nexus in the sky. The vortex of stream energy pulsed once, then began to sing—a complex, layered harmony of a billion individual voices, all unified in a single, defiant purpose.

Across the galaxy, every Kryll felt it. On flagships and in colonial bunkers, soldiers and civilians alike stopped. They felt a new strength flow into them, a clarity, a connection not just to the stream, but to each other. They were no longer just an echo of the past. They were a living, breathing verse of the present.

But the new song did not go unanswered.

From the deepest void, the Devourers turned their attention. They saw not a deviation to be corrected, but a rival law of reality to be erased.

From the fissure above Nevaris, a fleet of black, razor-shaped ships poured forth.

Aboard the *Crimson Corsair*, Admiral Vekzara watched the holomap ignite. "They're coming," he said, his voice quiet. "All of them." He looked at the faces of his crew, no longer seeing soldiers, but seeing the future of a species that had just chosen to fight for its own existence.

"To every ship in the Imperium," Vekzara broadcasted, his voice ringing with a strength he hadn't felt in decades. "We have made our choice. Now we fight for it. For Xylar. For the Imperium. For our right to sing our own song!"

The final battle had begun.

The sky above Xylos became a storm of light and shadow. The Devourer fleet moved with silent, geometric precision, their weapons erasing whatever they touched. But the Kryll fleet, now imbued with a new power of resonance, met them head-on. Ships shimmered with harmonic shields, weapons fired lances of pure, focused sound.

On the ground of the ghost planet, Xylar was transformed. The glyph on his chest blazed like a star. He was no longer just a soldier; he was the anchor of his people's new reality. He rose into the air, a being of flesh and energy, and met the Devourer vanguard as they descended.

The battle was not one of tactics, but of will. Of two fundamental truths of the universe colliding.

Chapter 25: Crimson Dawn

The war was short, brutal, and absolute. When the final Devourer ship dissolved into nothingness under a combined harmonic blast from the entire Kryll fleet, a new silence fell. Not the silence of absence, but the quiet of an ended conflict.

In the aftermath, a new Kryll Imperium was born. They were no longer just soldiers; they were custodians of a new kind of power, their society rebuilt around the harmony of individuality and unity.

Admiral Vekzara, his guilt finally absolved in the fires of the final battle, oversaw the creation of a new Council, one that included scientists, artists, and historians alongside warriors.

Gheda became the first Keeper of the Spiral Throne, dedicated to studying the infinite possibilities of the stream and ensuring their history would never again be forgotten.

And Xylar...

He stood on a ridge on Xylos Prime, the now-familiar crimson sun rising at his back. The glyph on his chest had faded to a subtle, silvery tracery, a permanent part of him. He was no longer a Herald or a warrior, just... himself.

Gheda and Valerius approached, their armor shed for simple robes.

"They're calling you a hero," Valerius said. "A god, some of them."

Xylar watched the sunrise. "I was just a soldier who remembered the mission," he said.

"And what's the mission now?" Gheda asked.

Xylar looked at the horizon, at the endless possibilities of a future they had earned. For the first time in his long life, he didn't have an answer. And the not knowing felt like peace.

"To keep singing," he said. "Just to keep singing."

The new day dawned, crimson and full of promise, and for the first time in recorded history, the Kryll were truly free.

Acknowledgeme

This book could not have been written in isolation—nor should any story of war, memory, and redemption be. I am indebted to those who lent their voices, insights, and encouragement through the long, winding path of this novel.

To the storytellers who inspired me to ask what lies beyond the stars—and what lies buried within ourselves—your echoes resonate on every page.

To my early readers and critics, whose sharp eyes and sharper minds helped sculpt the chaos into something clear, compelling, and true.

To the architects of worlds—both fictional and real—who showed me that a galaxy's worth of wonder can unfold from a single question well asked.

To my family and friends, who gave me the space to disappear into this world and the grace to return from it.

And finally, to the readers who carry this story forward—your curiosity is the spark, your imagination the fuel. Thank you for stepping into the breach.

About the Author

Jason Thomson writes speculative fiction that explores the intersections of memory, identity, and the unknown. With a background in both science and storytelling, he crafts layered narratives that blend the awe of deep-space exploration with the emotional grit of those who dare to question what came before.

When he's not unraveling ancient alien conspiracies or charting star systems on a napkin, Jason can be found hiking remote trails, losing track of time in planetariums, or debating the ethics of AI over too much coffee. The Swarm War is his latest journey into the void—and the human (or inhuman) truths hidden within it.

He believes the best stories don't just entertain—they echo.

To see more of Jason's publications, please visit his coming-soon web site at:

http://wwww.JasonThomsonBooks.com